ALL THIS AND WO

The psychology of o

ALL THIS
AND WORK TOO

The psychology of office life

DR MARYON TYSOE

Fontana/Collins

First published in 1988 by Fontana Paperbacks
8 Grafton Street, London W1X 3LA

Printed and bound in Great Britain by
William Collins Sons & Co. Ltd, Glasgow

For my parents
with love

CONTENTS

ACKNOWLEDGEMENTS

Authors' acknowledgements are so often like those extremely unconvincing Oscar acceptance speeches, where the recipient thanks every single human being he or she has ever met, plus the cat.

Notwithstanding, I honestly *do* want to thank: Helen Fraser, formerly of Fontana, for commissioning this book in the first place; Mike Fishwick, my editor, and Vivien Green, my agent, for their unfailing support and encouragement; John Denny, my excellent copy editor; and Alex Howell and everyone else at Fontana who have made the tortuous process of producing a book so much less painful than it might have been. Lastly, I would like to thank my friends and family who, as they say with a long-suffering moan, 'lived with this' for months . . .

I am grateful to the following for permission to quote from copyright material. In the case of some extracts, the wording has been slightly changed for ease of reading.

Academic Press and Philip M. Podsakoff for quote on pp. 60–62, from P. M. Podsakoff, W. D. Todor, R. A. Grover and V. L. Huber, 'Situational moderators of leader reward and punishment behaviors: fact or fiction?', *Organizational Behavior and Human Performance*, 34 (1984), 21–63.

The extracts on pp. 43 and 44 are reprinted from 'Coping with Cupid: the formation, impact, and management of romantic relationships in organizations' by R. E. Quinn, published in *Administrative Science Quarterly*, 22(1), March 1977, 30–45, by permission of *Administrative Science Quarterly*. © Cornell University.

Carolyn Aldwyn, Richard Lazarus and the American Psychological Association for quote on p. 153, from C. M. Aldwin and T. A. Revenson, 'Does coping help? A reexamination of the relation between coping and mental health', *Journal of Personality and Social Psychology*, **53** (1987), 337–48

Century Hutchinson and Barrie and Jenkins (now an imprint of Century Hutchinson) for quote on pp. 14–15, from P. G. Wodehouse, *Psmith in the City* (Penguin, 1970).

Cary Cooper and Fontana for quotes on pp. 91, 141–2, 158–9, 168, and 174, from C. Cooper and M. Davidson, *High Pressure*, 1982.

William Heinemann Ltd for quotes on pp. 31, 32–3, 34 and 79–80, from M. Argyle and M. Henderson, *The Anatomy of Relationships* (Penguin, 1985).

The Controller of Her Majesty's Stationery Office for the table on p. 170, taken from Table 10.1 of *Social Trends* 17, 1987.

David Kipnis and the American Psychological Association for quotes on pp. 88 and 89, from D. Kipnis, S. M. Schmidt and I. Wilkinson, 'Intraorganizational influence tactics: explorations in getting one's way', *Journal of Applied Psychology*, **65** (1980), 440–52.

Charles E. Merrill Publishing Company for quotes on pp. 85–6, 140, 155 and 161–2, from A. L. Appell, *A Practical Approach to Human Behavior in Business*, 1984.

New Society for the use of parts of some of my own published articles.

Plenum Publishing Corporation for the table on pp. 136–7, from J. Hall and W. H. Watson, 'The effects of a normative intervention on group decision-making performance', *Human Relations*, **23** (1970), 299–317.

Sage Publications for quote on p. 32, from M. Argyle and M. Henderson, 'The rules of relationships', chapter in S. Duck and D. Perlman (eds.), *Understanding Personal Relationships*, 1985.

Terri A. Scandura and the American Psychological Association for quotes on pp. 49–50, 50–51 and 51–2, from T. A. Scandura and G. B. Graen, 'Moderating effects of initial leader-member exchange status on the effects of a leadership intervention', *Journal of Applied Psychology*, **69** (1984), 428–36.

Thames Methuen for quotes on pp. 156, 161, 162 and 173–4, from M. Lucas, K. Wilson and E. Hart, *How to Survive the 9–5*, 1986.

The extracts on pp. 54–5 and 55–7 are reprinted from *Leadership and Decision-Making* by Victor H. Vroom and Philip W. Yetton by permission of the University of Pittsburgh Press. © 1973 by University of Pittsburgh Press. I originally located these extracts in the following paper: V. H. Vroom and A. G. Jago, 'On the validity of the Vroom–Yetton model', *Journal of Applied Psychology*, **63** (1978), 151–62. Copyright 1978 by the American Psychological Association. Adapted by permission of the publisher and author.

Every effort has been made to obtain all necessary permissions to reproduce copyright material throughout this book. If any proper acknowledgement has not been made, or permission not received, I apologise and invite any copyright holder to inform the publisher and myself of this oversight.

1

Into the maelstrom

It's 7.30 a.m. The alarm penetrates your dreams like the Last Trump. Groaning, plunging out of bed, foaming soap and toothpaste, rootling indecisively in the wardrobe . . . reeling, awash with instant coffee, out of the front door . . . Yes, you're on your way to The Office.

> Who first invented Work – and tied the free
> And holy-day rejoicing spirit down
> To the ever-haunting importunity
> Of business, in the green fields and the town –
> To plough – loom – anvil – spade – and, oh, most sad,
> To this dry drudgery of the desk's dead wood?[1]

Charles Lamb, here, being a bit savage about The Office in 1822. Mind you, you don't get too much of the 'desk's dead wood' in today's offices – it's all gleaming beech and polished rubber-plants and shiny red wastepaper baskets with matching designer in-trays.

And as for the 'dry drudgery' . . .

The popular image of the office, even now, is that it's just so *dull*. Eight hours of quiet paper-rustling, interrupted by the odd spasm of violent paper-shuffling, visits to the coffee dispenser and the lunchtime sandwich.

This is nonsense, of course. The office is a maelstrom of intrigue, rivalry, hate, upset, indifference, jealousy, scapegoating, boredom, pressure and imminent catastrophe; as well as of triumph, pleasure, satisfaction, friendship and even love. And that's on top of the work . . .

'We wise grown-ups here at the company,' wrote novelist

Joseph Heller in his satire *Something Happened*, 'go gliding in and out all day long, scaring each other at our desks and cubicles and water coolers and trying to evade the people who frighten us. We come to work, have lunch, and go home. We goose-step in and goose-step out, change our partners and wander all about, sashay around for a pat on the head, and promenade home till we all drop dead.'

But Heller's hero does admit, albeit reluctantly, that there's more to it than that. 'I find I am being groomed for a better job. And I find – God help me – that I want it.'[2]

The urge to get the most out of your working life is of course perfectly sensible – after all, we spend about a third of our waking hours earning a crust. And work does matter to us. One British survey of full-time employees found that 69 per cent of men and 65 per cent of women would continue to work even if it were no longer financially necessary.[3] Work provides a lot of things besides money: the chance to achieve, a structure to life, security, a position in society – and companionship. In fact, you'll see more of your boss, colleagues and subordinates than you will of your friends and relations.

As we all know, this is not always an unmixed pleasure. Bosses, in particular, seem to be a prime focus of office horror stories.

In one of his early novels, *Psmith in the City* (1910), P. G. Wodehouse describes a certain Mr Bickersdyke, manager of the New Asiatic Bank:

The staff had known him to be in a bad temper before – frequently; but his frame of mind on all previous occasions had been, compared with his present frame of mind, that of a rather exceptionally good-natured lamb. Within ten minutes of his arrival the entire office was on the jump. The messengers were collected in a pallid group in the basement, discussing the affair in whispers and endeavouring to restore their nerve with about sixpenn'orth of the beverage known as 'unsweetened'. The heads of departments, to a man, had bowed before the storm. Within the space of seven minutes and a quarter Mr Bickersdyke had contrived to find some fault with each of them. Inward Bills was out at an A.B.C. shop snatching a hasty cup of coffee, to pull him together again. Outward Bills was sitting at his desk with the glazed stare of one who has been struck in the thorax by a thunderbolt. Mr Rossiter had been torn from Psmith in the middle of a highly technical discussion of the Manchester United match, just as he was showing – with the aid of a ball of paper – how he had once seen Meredith centre to Sandy Turnbull in a Cup match, and was now leaping about like a distracted grasshopper. Mr Waller, head of the Cash Department, had been summoned to the Presence, and after listening meekly to a rush of criticism, had retired to his desk with the air of a beaten spaniel.[4]

Frightful bosses do not just lurk in the safe pages of novels, unfortunately. A friend of mine told me about his:

My boss is what is known technically as a paranoid schizophrenic. He constantly feels that people are trying to get the better of him, and this makes him very aggressive and hostile. You can sense the hostility welling up in him whenever you disagree with him about anything. He might say it's cold, and you say actually you think it's quite warm, and that's it. He swells up and his eyes narrow. I've been at staff meetings where I *know* every single person disagrees with what he's saying, and not one will speak out. Because he'll be so vile, and you'll be churned up for the whole day. Besides, you know he's going to make the decision in the end anyway, so what's the point.

Even with a good boss, the mere mention of the words 'meeting' and 'committee' tends to bring a moan to one's lips, and satirical souls can have a field day with them:

Meetings: 'Indispensable when you don't want to do anything' (J. K. Galbraith).

Committees: 'A group that takes minutes and wastes hours' (Anon.);

'A group of the unfit appointed by the unwilling to do the unnecessary' (Carl C. Byers);

'We always carry out by committee anything in which any of us alone would be too reasonable to persist' (Frank Moore Colby);

'To get something done a committee should consist of no more than three men, two of whom are absent' (Robert Copeland).[5]

Sexist, that last one; but then there's still quite a lot of that about. For women, it adds yet another work pressure. And there are quite enough pressures as it is, thanks to the likes of the fictional Mr Bickersdyke and my friend's all-too-real boss.

So how are we to deal with the vital soap opera we call office life and emerge happier, more in control – perhaps more successful too?

There has been plenty of research by psychologists which is relevant to the way we conduct ourselves at work. What I have done is to mine it for the most useful themes and findings, which I believe can help people to make the most of their working lives.

This book is designed for *everyone* who works in an office, whatever their status. After all, the basic psychological issues remain the same whatever level of the hierarchy you occupy.

In chapter 2 I'm going to look at the pervasive question of Colleagues – from how to build good relationships with them and avoid bad ones, through the agonies of sexual harassment and the problems of office love-affairs, to the minutiae of how you present yourself – whether we like it or not, that matters too. The *Punch* cartoon of an angry boss saying to a young man in an appallingly knotted tie, 'Good Heavens,

Adkins! Didn't they teach you *anything* at the Harvard Business School?' really hit the nail on the head.

Chapter 3 is on dealing with your subordinates – how to motivate them to work well *and* happily for you. Don't say 'Well, gosh, I'm not a top dog – that can't apply to me.' The same principles apply whether the only person beneath you is the one-seventeenth of a secretary that you share with the rest of your department or whether you direct a cast of thousands.

Chapter 4 tackles Bosses – how to handle them, how to get on with them, how to assert yourself when necessary; and the importance of not threatening their status. Another perceptive *Punch* cartoon depicts a severe, besuited man standing in the doorway of a junior executive's thickly carpeted office, clutching a scythe and saying, 'Nobody has a deeper pile than J.B., young man.'[6]

Chapter 5 examines the vexed question of how to make effective decisions and be creative, either on your own or in a group. Group decision-making, as we've already seen, is an easy target if you're feeling in a sarcastic mood. But it doesn't have to be as awful as it all too frequently is.

In chapter 6 we consider ways of presenting your views effectively and being taken seriously; and how to avoid being manipulated by the unscrupulous. 'Oh, come on, won't you do it just this *once*.' Know the sort of thing?

Chapter 7 is about strategies for dealing with stress, the great bugbear of office life. 'I have a new philosophy,' says a character in a *Peanuts* cartoon. 'I'm only going to dread one day at a time.' But seriously, we can do a lot better than that.

Finally, chapter 8 looks at 'getting on' – or not, as the case may be. At how you can stop handicapping yourself by negative thinking; and at how, in the last analysis, 'getting on' is only part of the work experience – and work is only part of life. Let's get the thing in perspective.

This is not a treatise on manipulating others, nor is it

dedicated to handy hints on clawing your way to the top. In essence, if you're a warm, assertive and competent person, I think you'll have a far better working life than if you're a backstabbing, bullshitting bastard. Those sorts of people can make the odd short-term gain, but you'll be the one who does well in the long term – and I suspect you'll be a lot happier too.

This book is therefore about understanding how you and other people tick, how you can make the best of yourself, and how to smooth your path with others and make your working life – and theirs – more pleasant and productive.

2

Colleagues – how to get on with them

I have terrible trouble with Keith. He's always bitching at me and being obstructive. I simply can't understand it.

Sue always makes me feel uncomfortable. I'm not the only one, either. No one ever seems to ask her to lunch – I feel a bit sorry for her, really.

Jenny's great. If it weren't for her sitting at the next desk, someone to have a laugh with, I don't think I'd stick it.

Colleagues. There's no getting away from them, is there? You spend about a third of your waking time in their company each week – whether you like them or not.

How can you make the very best of it? In this chapter we're going to look at ways you can smooth your path through the rocky terrain of relationships at work.

Let's start with the basics. How do you come across to other people?

THE WAY YOU LOOK

I know, I know. Thinking about this sort of thing reminds you of your mother. 'You can't go out like that, dear. What will people think?'

Physical attractiveness

The unfortunate truth is that physical appearance does matter – perhaps more than we like to think. 'Beauty,' wrote

Aristotle, 'is a greater recommendation than any letter of introduction.'

And how right he was. Psychologists have exhausted themselves measuring the responses of hundreds of people – usually American university students, the handiest group of people to study – to photographs of attractive and unattractive people. Attractiveness, in case you're wondering, is typically rated by groups of volunteer judges. They tend to agree on who is attractive and who is not.

Good looks, good personality? What researchers usually find is that the good-lookers are thought to have more attractive personalities – being more 'poised, interesting, sociable, independent, exciting and sexually warm'.[1]

Their work may be considered better, too. In an experiment in which male students were asked to judge essays written by women, the essays supposedly written by attractive women were rated higher than identical essays supposedly by unattractive ones.[2]

But do not immediately rush to your mirror and wonder how you've managed to get through life so far.

In an office you have a chance to get to know people over time – bumping into them by the office kettle, borrowing their pencil sharpeners, waiting in line for the photocopier – and you gather a lot more information about them than what their faces look like. Jeff from Admin might not score many points out of ten in the Harrison Ford glamour stakes, but he might be frightfully bright, kind to his mother and go hanggliding at the weekends. But you'd never find out about his intelligence, kindness and predilection for exotic sports if you didn't bother to get into conversation with him in the first place. The danger is that we make snap judgements about people at first sight and, if we're not taken by the way they look, we might never approach them at all.

Self-fulfilling prophecies. When we make those extremely swift initial judgements, the way a person looks is one of the crucial pieces of information we have at that point. If he or she is physically attractive – what social scientists call a 'culturally desirable' characteristic – we may, without being very aware of it, be nicer to them.

Awful as it sounds, psychologists have evidence that this is often true. One classic experiment demonstrated the point perfectly. A team of American social psychologists, Mark Snyder, Elizabeth Tanke and Ellen Berscheid, told male students that they would be having a telephone conversation with a woman who was either 'attractive' or 'unattractive'. (In reality, the women in both samples had been rated by judges as being equally attractive.)

Results showed that the men who thought they were talking to an attractive woman were more sociable and socially adept than if they thought she was unattractive. What's more, judges rating the woman's part of the conversation found her to be more friendly, likeable and sociable when the man on the other end of the line was (unknown to her) under the impression that she was good-looking.[3]

Although this experiment looked just at men talking to women, it illustrates precisely how a self-fulfilling prophecy can work – the men behaved in such a way that their stereotyped preconceptions about their conversational partner came true.

Social self-confidence. Psychologists have paid remarkably little attention to the long-term effects on personality and behaviour of being attractive, but there is some evidence that the attractive are more socially self-confident[4] and (although the evidence isn't conclusive for this) socially skilled[5] than the less attractive. They also enjoy more satisfactory and pleasurable interactions with others than do the more homely-looking.[6] But there are no very clear indications that the attractive and unattractive differ in any other major respect.

So what are the implications? There are two lessons to be learned from all this:

1. Don't make any premature judgements about any of your colleagues on the basis of the way they look. People always deny that they judge a book by its cover, but the evidence is that appearance can colour first impressions, and people can either act in such a way that they make that impression come true, or interpret the other person's behaviour to make it fit in with their initial judgements.

With colleagues you talk to every day because they sit next to you or you have to work on projects together, the way they look will have diminishing importance for you. But with more distant colleagues, who might require an effort to get to know, don't let rather unprepossessing looks put you off. Which of us hasn't had the experience of meeting someone at our office leaving party and wishing we'd bothered to get to know them before?

2. The way *you* look makes some difference. This applies to men as well as women. It is unfair that this should be so, but, knowing that it is so, you can decide whether or not to act upon it – if you don't already.

What to do? If you want to make yourself more attractive, how do you go about it? What makes a person attractive anyway?

For all their physical attractiveness studies, psychologists have paid little attention to the real differences between those judged attractive and those not. But two American sociologists, Murray Webster and James Driskell, have done just this. They selected for their study eight photographs of attractive and unattractive students from over 800 pictures. The eight were thought to be representative of the normal range of attractiveness among college students. 'Yet,' Webster and Driskell say, 'there is no obvious characteristic that either the attractive or the unattractive ones have in common . . .

The overall impression from these pictures is that very minor and superficial changes in hairstyle, weight, and, perhaps, clothing would be sufficient to make the unattractive people more attractive, or the reverse.'[7]

This is hardly a very scientific observation, but interesting none the less. There is certainly evidence that obesity is seen as unattractive,[8] and so are sad expressions.[9] When psychologists have occasionally done studies that have used the same people in both the unattractive and the attractive photos, they have typically been women and the changes have been wrought entirely by make-up and hairstyling.[10] Research has shown that correctly applied make-up does make women more attractive – women's beliefs that this is so are entirely accurate.[11]

But many women dislike the idea of make-up, and it is important to emphasize at this point that none of these things is utterly vital. It's simply that appearance has subtle and often insidious effects, and it's better to be aware of them than not.

You can boost the way you appear to others by one other technique. In an intriguing study, students rated an instructor after a seven-minute interview. The instructor was always the same person, but in some interviews he tried to be likeable and in others rather cold. The students thought him more *physically* attractive when he was likeable . . .[12]

Clothes

Webster and Driskell tell the story that the sociologist Talcott Parsons's advice to one student was: 'Since you intend to revolutionize sociology, and perhaps society, let me offer one suggestion. Wear a tie. You can sneak up on them that way.'[13]

Research on clothes, like the physical attractiveness work, has concentrated on the impression given at first sight. One American study had personnel administrators viewing silent videotapes of women being interviewed for a management job, wearing different outfits of varying degrees of 'masculinity':

> *Costume 1.* A light beige dress in a soft fabric, with a small round collar, gathered skirt, and long sleeves (least masculine costume).
>
> *Costume 2.* A bright aqua suit with a short belted jacket and a white blouse with a large, softly draped bow at the neck.
>
> *Costume 3.* A beige, tailored suit with a blazer jacket and a rust blouse with a narrow bow at the neck.
>
> *Costume 4.* A dark navy, tailored suit and a white blouse with an angular collar (most masculine costume).

The researchers found that with increasing masculinity, from costumes 1 to 3, the administrators' hiring recommendations were increasingly favourable. But for costume 4, the most masculine, favourability dropped again down to that associated with costume 2. For these personnel selectors, the researchers say, costume 4 'may have been perceived as too masculine to be appropriate for women'.[14]

That, however, is a matter of style and fashion. But the basic point – that the more masculine the better – is the crucial one. Management posts are, even these days, stereotyped as 'masculine' – as are many positions in professional and business life. Although the costume study quoted was artificial, the findings fit in with those of research specifically on the role of attractiveness at work.

Appearances at work

The research I have described so far all supports the 'what is beautiful is good' stereotype.[15] But this principle may not always hold – sometimes one can get the 'beauty is beastly' effect.[16]

Research has shown that when you simulate hiring decisions, attractive men are preferred to equally qualified but unattractive men for both non-managerial and managerial jobs. But while attractive women are preferred to unattractive ones for traditionally feminine, non-managerial jobs, or for managerial positions where 'good interpersonal skills' are a central requirement,[17] this is not the case for management posts where stereotypically 'masculine' skills such as leadership and decision-making are emphasized. Here, unattractive women have the edge over attractive ones.[18]

But how can this be, when research has shown that attractive people are seen not only as more socially skilled but also more competent at tasks that have nothing to do with looks, such as flying a plane?[19]

The answer seems to be that physically attractive men are seen as more masculine than less attractive ones, and masculinity is 'culturally desirable' for both kinds of jobs. Similarly, attractive women are seen as more feminine than unattractive ones.[20] This is fine for low-status or 'feminine' jobs; *but it is not fine for posts where traditionally 'masculine' skills are at a premium.*

The message for men is plain. Whatever your job, looking smart, stylish and well groomed will do you no harm at all. In certain circumstances it might do you a lot of good. For example, if you're meeting clients, visitors, new colleagues or the boss for the first time, or if you want to be noticed favourably in a large office.

But women, in contrast, seem to have rather a dilemma. In general, looking good seems a reasonable plan. But if you want to impress in any job classed as 'masculine', it may not be such a wonderful idea.

The way to resolve this dilemma seems fairly clear. Looking as good as you can is fine as long as you don't swan around in softly draped dresses and masses of make-up. In other words, avoid the 'super-feminine' look. If you are in a classically female job, like a secretary, but you have aspirations to higher things, splash out on a sharp suit too.

All these things may seem trivial, but don't underestimate them. I once interviewed a charming woman two years after she had had a one-day professional makeover (face, hair, clothes), and she told me it had literally changed her life for the better. She felt much more positive about herself, was going to university as a mature student – the works. Although I knew about the research in this area, I was staggered that a one-off experience could have such deep-rooted effects – *simply by increasing her self-confidence*.

So don't dismiss the effect of physical appearance, on yourself or other people; but don't become obsessed by it either. People use many criteria when they judge you as a person, and appearance is only one, even if it is one that has a disproportionate effect on people's first impressions.

THE WAY YOUR OFFICE SPACE LOOKS

OK, so there you are, looking sharp, feeling good. Now let's look around you. Is your desk completely invisible beneath a pile of curling papers, cigarette ends and the greasy paper bag that held yesterday's egg sandwich? Or is it completely empty save for your designer pen-holder, pristine note-pad and quietly glinting computer terminal?

Your personal office space is part of your image. Research shows that people will draw conclusions about you on the basis of the way your office looks. As with the effects of physical appearance, it matters more with people who don't know you well: visitors, clients, people higher up the hierarchy whom you rarely see.

So why not create the impression that you want to convey?

Tidiness

Tidiness seems to be a crucial factor. In one study university lecturers were shown colour slides of faculty offices and then asked about their reactions and their deductions about the

occupants. There were three levels of tidiness: clean, inter-
mediate ('organized stacks') and messy. Occupants of the
messy offices were thought to be the most busy, least
organized and most extrovert; inhabitants of the clean offices
were regarded as the most organized and the least busy. But
the real winner seemed to be the office where papers and
other materials were in organized piles. This was seen as most
welcoming and comfortable, and the occupant was seen as
the highest in rank and achievement, only slightly less busy
than the occupant of the messy office, and an awful lot more
organized.[21]

Seating arrangements

The state of your desk and work surfaces is something you
can do something about. Other aspects of your work-space,
like the position of your desk, you may not be able to alter,
either because there's only one place it can be, or because you
work for the sort of organization that would come down on
you like a ton of bricks for fiddling with their designer layout.

But if you have a bit of leeway, the evidence is that an
'open desk arrangement' (desk against wall) is seen as more
comfortable and welcoming, and the occupant as more acces-
sible, friendly, extrovert and confident in dealing with others
than is the case with a 'closed' arrangement (desk as a barrier
between you and everyone else).[22] Plants and posters, too,
give the place an inviting feel.[23]

PRIVACY

Sometimes, of course, you might feel anything but welcoming. Many offices these days are open-plan, and studies show
that lack of privacy, interruptions and disturbances are
common problems.[24]

Ronald Goodrich, an American 'behavioral consultant',
interviewed employees at the firm ARCO who occupied
open-plan work-stations:

They complained that people would penetrate what they defined as their personal workspace and walk right up to their desk. They experienced this as an intrusion, a breach of their personal space, and an invasion of their privacy. They also felt some powerlessness due to their inability to control access to and the use of their space.

Their reactions to this were really quite severe. Goodrich says:

> Workers reported that conflict for the individual and mutual misunderstanding may result if the desire for privacy is not clearly stated physically, nonverbally, or verbally. They described being annoyed with the other person, feared alienating the other person by asking him to leave once he was there, and felt some anxiety about being unable to complete their work as a result.[25]

The message is clear. Try not to interrupt colleagues unless absolutely necessary; i.e. try to restrain yourself from yelling 'Hey, did you *see* that awful play on the telly last night?' over the partition to your work neighbour, who at that precise moment has just written 'And in conclusion . . .' and is chewing her pen in an agony of indecision. If you do have to speak to someone, don't go too close until you're sure you are welcome.

Personal space

Researchers have found that we are all surrounded by an invisible bubble, called our 'personal space' in the jargon.[26] The size of this bubble varies according to the situation we are in. The evidence is that in America – and this seems applicable to the British too – there are four distances we normally adopt when talking to people:

1. *Intimate distance* – zero to one and a half feet – is the distance appropriate for things like love-making, comforting and fighting.

2. *Personal distance* – one and a half to four feet – is used for everyday conversation among friends and acquaintances.

3. *Social distance* – four to twelve feet – is appropriate for business and other impersonal conversations. People who work together typically use the 'close phase' of social distance, four to seven feet.

4. *Public distance* – over twelve feet – is the distance usually used in formal settings, as when a speaker is addressing an audience.[27]

The evidence is that we feel uncomfortable if someone stands or sits at a distance inappropriate for our relationship or the circumstances. The American anthropologist who first noticed the four zones, Edward T. Hall, illustrated what can happen. He observed that, compared to the distance that Americans and Europeans feel comfortable with, Arabs and Latin Americans prefer to come in much closer when talking. Unfortunately from the American or European point of view, this 'invasion' of personal space is normally associated with hostile or sexual intent. Even if they know this is not really very likely, they still feel vaguely uncomfortable, and the automatic reaction is to back up, probably thinking 'What an aggressive, pushy person this is.'

The comfortable distance for westerners can, however, be very hurtful to the Arabs and Latin Americans. 'What have I done?' . . . 'Doesn't he like me?' are their likely interpretations. And they will probably move in again so they can feel at ease, meanwhile, perhaps, thinking 'What a cold, distant, unfriendly person *this* is.'

The results can be quite dramatic. Hall recounts tales of American diplomats at international receptions retreating backwards down corridors, gyrating in circles and being pinned against walls by other diplomats who are simply trying to establish their habitual talking distance.[28]

Reactions may be even worse with members of one's own culture, who 'ought to know better'. It's clear that it is important not to stand too close if your relationship doesn't justify it, and not to move in too close while they're sitting at their desks. Once you've moved into the 'personal distance' zone, they may feel obliged to talk to you whether they want to or not.

The best plan would be to stand at the near end of 'social distance' – i.e., about four to five feet – and ask if it's a bad moment, say you can come back later, that you only wanted to ask them about the Kittyfood account. If they say it's OK, then move in to a comfortable distance. Given the strains of frequent interruptions placed on people in open-plan offices – and not necessarily just in open-plan offices, either – such considerate tactics will do you nothing but good.

Self-protection

If, for example, you're working desperately hard on something and can't handle interruptions, *say so immediately*. Don't let them start telling you that they've just discovered that Kittyfood gives off toxic fumes and glows in the dark and what the hell are they going to do, and then cut them off. It's very important for people to feel good about themselves, and being snubbed by you is not going to increase your popularity quotient. Similarly with the ostrich technique – the 'I'll keep staring at my desk while they're talking to me and perhaps if I don't look at them they'll disappear' method. They will, but thinking dark thoughts.

Just look up as they approach, and say 'Fred, hi, I'm in a desperate state here, is it absolutely vital or can I come and talk to you later?' If Fred is a monumental pain in the neck who always arrives to see you at 11.06 a.m. just when you're feeling that if you don't get to the coffee machine in the next six seconds you're going to die, then add riders like 'Mornings are usually *awful* times for me', or 'I'm sorry, I'm always so buried in the mornings', until he gets the message. Without having his feelings hurt.

RULES OF RELATIONSHIPS

Getting on well with colleagues, as anyone who works in an office knows, is a vital element in our working lives. Many office jobs involve a great deal of time spent talking. One British study of 160 managers, for example, found that they spent between one third and 90 per cent of their time with other people.[29]

'Working relationships,' write Oxford social psychologists Michael Argyle and Monika Henderson, 'are first brought about by the formal system of work, but are elaborated in several ways by informal contacts of different kinds ... It is essential for such relationships to develop if co-operation at work is to succeed.'[30] And good relationships at work, research shows, are one of the main sources of job satisfaction[31] and well-being.[32]

Are there any 'rules of relationships' that might be useful as general markers of what to do and what not to do in your dealings with others?

'Universal' rules

Michael Argyle and his colleagues have found that there are such rules. Through interviews with people they generated a number of possible rules. Then they asked others to rate how important those rules were in twenty-two different kinds of relationships. These included relationships with spouses, close friends, siblings and work colleagues as well as relationships between work subordinates and their superiors.

The researchers discovered six 'universal' rules that applied to over half of all these relationships (the number in brackets is the number of kinds of relationships for which people said the rule was important):

1. Respect the other's privacy (22)
2. Look the other person in the eye during conversation (21)
3. Do not discuss what has been said in confidence with the other person (21)
4. Do/do not (as the relationship requires) indulge in sexual activity with the other person (14)
5. Do not criticize the other person publicly (13)
6. Repay debts, favours or compliments no matter how small (12)[33]

This doesn't mean that nobody breaks these rules, as we all know – it just means that they are seen as important. The 'looking in the eye' rule, for example, is a crucial aspect of good social skills.[34] It is very uncomfortable to have to talk to someone who never, or hardly ever, looks at you during the conversation. One needs to look at the person one is talking to to see if they're still attending and to monitor their reactions (if they've completely stopped looking at you and appear transfixed by the begonias in the window-box, it means shut up). To signal interest, the listener has to look quite frequently at the person who is speaking.

Work rules

As well as these general guidelines for keeping good relationships, Argyle and his associates questioned people about rules that apply very specifically to work settings. In addition to the 'universal' rules they came up with nine 'rules for co-workers':

1. Accept one's fair share of the workload.
2. Be cooperative with regard to the shared physical working conditions (e.g. light, temperature, noise).
3. Be willing to help when requested.
4. Work cooperatively despite feelings of dislike.

5. Don't denigrate co-workers to superiors.
6. Address the co-worker by first name.
7. Ask for help and advice when necessary.
8. Don't be over-inquisitive about each other's private lives.
9. Stand up for the co-worker in his/her absence.[35]

Again, these make a lot of sense. And number 4 is an interesting one – it raises the big problem of colleagues with whom you simply don't get on. In one of their studies, Monika Henderson, Michael Argyle and co-workers defined four categories of work relationships:

1. *Social friends*: 'friends in the normal sense who are known through work and seen at social events outside the work setting'. Research shows that up to a quarter of friends are made through work.

2. *Friends at work*: 'friends who interact together over work or socially at work, but who are not invited home and do not engage in joint leisure activities outside the work setting'.

3. *Work-mates*: 'people at work seen simply through formal work contacts and with whom interactions are relatively superficial and task-oriented, and not characterised by either liking or dislike'.

4. *Conflict relations*: 'work colleagues who are actively disliked'.[36]

This last is a tricky one. What to do? Just imagine the scene:

BOSS: 'Come *in*, Ms Simmonds. We've just landed a new client who is going to need the *utmost* attention. I thought I'd assign both you and Kevin here to the job. I'm sure you'll make a great team. It'll mean long hours, I'm afraid.'

Ms S. and Kevin, suppressing their glances of mutual loathing, grin weakly and shuffle out into a dim future of murky misery.

Disliked colleagues

Argyle and Co., undaunted by even this sort of difficulty, have come up with a special list of endorsed 'rules for people we can't get on with'. The main ones are:

1. Respect each other's privacy.
2. Strive to be fair in relations with one another.
3. Don't discuss what is said in confidence.
4. Don't feel free to take up as much of the other's time as one desires.
5. Don't denigrate the other behind their back.
6. Don't ignore the other person.
7. Repay debts, favours or compliments no matter how small.
8. Look the other person in the eye during conversation.
9. Don't display hypocritical liking.[37]

There are also a couple of others that seem a touch unnecessary, like don't invite them to dine at a family celebration and don't have sex with them. I mean, is one likely to?

Argyle and Henderson also suggest: 'Another approach to resolving interpersonal conflicts is increasing the amount of communication between those involved, so that each side comes to understand and to trust the other more. Suspicion and hostility are increased by ignorance of what the other is up to.'

Trying to get to know the other person a bit more, if you can manage it, is really quite a good approach. You might find they're really not so bad after all.

But people tend to distort information to fit in with their prejudices.[38] If you see mean old George buying his secretary flowers, don't automatically assume that he must be wanting her to work overtime that night. Perhaps it's actually her birthday, and George not the tight-fisted horror story you thought he was.

It's sometimes hard to pin down why we don't like someone, or why they don't like us. But there are some general psychological principles which are always useful to bear in mind:

The self-fulfilling prophecy again. If, say, you've heard that Richard is a very difficult man, when you meet him you are likely to be cold and defensive. Richard, being only human, is likely to react badly to this – and Lo, what you expected has come true.

A small personal example: I remember once meeting a new neighbour, of whom I knew nothing, and being warm and pleasant to her from our first meeting. It wasn't (fortunately) until later that I heard of her reputation as an extremely prickly and uncooperative woman. But to me she was always kind, watered my plants when I was away, and kept an eye open for burglars.[39]

Errors of judgement. Psychologists have found that when we try to work out why someone is behaving in a certain way we frequently fall prey to what they call the 'fundamental attribution error'. That is, we tend to explain others' actions in terms of their personal dispositions rather than the situation in which they find themselves. As the American social psychologists Robert Baron and Donn Byrne put it, 'Often, we seem to perceive others as acting as they do largely because they are "that kind of person"; the many situational factors which may also have affected their behaviour tend to be ignored, or at least downplayed.'[40]

So if colleague A is constantly ratty, and colleague B always miserable, it may be doing them an injustice to conclude that A is simply a bad-tempered bitch and B a pathetic wimpish depressive. It may well be that things are going on in their lives of which you are completely unaware or whose importance you underestimate. A, perhaps, has to rush home every night to look after her ailing, nagging old mother, never has a jolly night out, or never got that promotion she thought was her due. B, meanwhile, is suffering from a series of appalling catastrophes. After months of suspicion he has just learned that his wife is having an affair, he has found some peculiar-looking white powder in the pocket of his teenage daughter's Levi 501s, and he's feeling very stuck in his job.

In other words these two colleagues are responding not unnaturally to their circumstances; it does not mean that they have appalling personalities. Psychologists think that behaviour is normally a product of the person *and* the situation[41] – so although not everyone reacts the same way to awful circumstances, it's important not to downplay the influence of those circumstances on the way people behave.

Thinking this way about irritable A and gloomy B might not make you want to be friends with them, but it might make them easier to tolerate. You might even manage to work out some of the reasons why they feel as they do, and this in itself can give you a key to improving your relationship with them. If, for example, you decide that one of the main reasons C is so touchy is that she feels undervalued around the office, then asking her advice a few times will not only perk her up but will make her soften towards you. Her advice, what's more, might turn out to be extremely useful.

Is it just you? What if a colleague is happy, charming and delightful with everybody – or nearly everybody – in the office except you? There are several possibilities here:

1. It's a straightforward personality clash. Probably the best thing to do is to follow the Argyle-style rules and try to rub along and cooperate on work matters as best you can.

2. It may be that your colleague feels threatened by you. The more similar their job is to yours, say, the more they might see you as a danger to their position and reputation. The best thing here is simply to try to minimize the competitive element, for example by asking for advice and informa-

tion and emphasizing your different skills and responsibilities where possible.

3. You got off on the wrong footing initially – perhaps through some sort of self-fulfilling prophecy, as discussed earlier. If you think that's what has happened, monitor your own behaviour towards them. Do you ostentatiously avoid them, speak coldly to them when you have to address them, never look them in the eye, and never say, 'Hey, that was a good point you made at the meeting this morning'?

It's vital to realize, in your dealings with people, how very important it is to us all to think well of ourselves. We have, as social psychologist John Turner puts it, a 'need for positive self-esteem'.[42] You will get on best with people if you try not to damage their self-identity, and to bolster it when you can do so genuinely and believably.

So if you think your own behaviour might be perpetuating an unfortunate cycle of dislike, try gradually (not too suddenly – it'll look extremely false and thoroughly suspicious) to change it to a warmer, more rewarding and less defensive style. The evidence is that we usually like those who seem to like us, and don't like those whom we don't think like us.[43] And none of these things is unalterable.

SEXUAL HARASSMENT

Of all the aspects of relationships between colleagues, sexual harassment must be one of the most unpleasant. The essence of such harassment is that it involves *unwanted* sexual advances – it does not refer to thrilling mutual flirtations over boiled cabbage in the office canteen.

Both men and women are harassed, but women much more frequently than men. A major American survey of 23,000 federal employees produced a remarkable 85 per cent response rate, and showed that 42 per cent of the women and 15 per cent of the men had been sexually harassed.[44] In

Britain, a survey of sixty women managers found that 52 per cent had experienced sexual harassment at work (and most of those not harassed were older, in senior positions or in predominantly female work environments).[45]

What is harassment? Harassment is usually taken to cover staring and leering; sexual, derogatory or demeaning remarks or jokes; 'sexually suggestive' pin-ups; touching, brushing against, pinching and grabbing; sexual propositions or demands; assault and rape.

Case studies bring even the milder-sounding types of harassment horribly to life. Journalist Sue Read, in her book *Sexual Harassment at Work*, quotes the case of Donna, an American sales correspondent whose office was directly across a glass hallway from her sales manager:

> He would wait until I was on the telephone with a customer, and then he would walk up to the glass, look down at my breasts and start licking his lips . . . He would walk by my desk, lean over, rub himself against me and whisper remarks like, 'My hands are itching to get at your breasts. I hope you never have a chest cold.'

The final straw came when Donna's mother rang her to say her father had had a heart attack. The manager was in her room and heard the conversation. Donna put the telephone down, crying, and he 'took hold of the back of my white shirt and said, "Did I ever tell you that white really turns me on? I really like the way you fill out your sweaters."' Donna left her job.[46]

Why does it happen? The cosy view that sexual harassment is really not a problem, that it's just a reflection of natural sexual attraction between men and women, is simply not supported by the evidence – at least in the case of women being harassed by men (the more usual pattern). The favourite explanation nowadays is that sexual harassment is about power. It is a way of keeping women 'in their place' and denying them the status of a true colleague.

A second possibility – not at all incompatible with the power one – is that treating women in sexual terms at work is a 'spillover' from the way men regard women outside work. Women's 'gender role' – the part women are expected to play in life – involves a strong sexual element. If this idea is correct, it implies that the more the fact that a worker is a woman is 'noticeable', the more likely they are to be sexually harassed. So women would be particularly likely to be harassed in male-dominated jobs and occupations (such as management), and in 'female' occupations (such as secretarial work) where the woman is surrounded by men doing other jobs.

Research supports this idea, and it implies that sexual harassment is less rife in 'integrated' work-places where equal numbers of men and women do the same job.[47]

Who are the harassers? The evidence is that co-workers are the harassers more frequently than bosses. Even though bosses clearly have more power to punish you for not complying than co-workers do, many victims are afraid that they will be made to suffer for rebuffing a co-worker. And they could be right – as we all know, colleagues can make our lives pretty unpleasant if they really put their minds to it.

For women, harassers are usually older, married men. But for men, while homosexual harassment does occur, the problem is most likely to stem from a younger, single woman – possibly as a clumsy attempt to express attraction.[48]

A few male harassers, too, may be doing it as a crude way of saying they are interested in someone (although where this is true they should stop instantly if they don't get the 'right' reaction). Psychologists have found that men are more likely to view interchanges between men and women in sexual terms. In one study, an American social psychologist, Antonia Abbey, had male and female subjects observe a man and a woman discussing their experiences of university life. She found, rather revealingly, that the men rated both the man and the woman as being more promiscuous and seductive than women did.[49] So friendliness on a woman's part may well be assumed by a man to denote sexual interest.

The situation is complicated by the fact that, since women are frequently in less powerful positions than men at work, they may sometimes try to increase their power and influence by using their sexuality. This is a dangerous game to play, however. Ultimately sexual power is, as one psychologist I know put it, 'an empty power'.

What to do? Being sexually harassed can have really bad effects: not just psychological, such as depression and nervous disorders, but also physical, like aches and pains, nausea and insomnia. There is also evidence that it can make people less motivated to work and can damage the quality of their performance. Harassment can, as in Donna's case, drive them out of their jobs.[50]

So what can you do about it if it happens to you?

Researchers find that victims' usual reactions to being harassed are to avoid the harassers, to pretend to ignore their behaviour, or to act 'cool and guarded'.[51] Sadly, these techniques are not greatly effective in getting the harasser to lay off. The best technique at a personal level appears to be to assert yourself and to make *very clear* what you find offensive.[52] Do it in a joking fashion if you have to, but make sure they understand you mean it. 'Don't *do* that, you horrible man!' 'I bet you wouldn't treat Fred like that.' 'What's the matter, trying to get back at me because the boss liked my treatment better than yours?' 'Yes, well, I wish I could say the same about your legs.'

Victims' most commonly reported reactions to harassment are anger and embarrassment.[53] The normal reason for hiding these feelings is fear of retaliation. With co-workers, as this is less of a problem than with bosses, if joking doesn't work the best plan is probably to express your feelings plainly. With your boss, if you can't face doing that directly try the 'I never mix business with pleasure, I find it impossible to be taken seriously as a fellow worker otherwise, it would ruin our working relationship' type of tactics.

One recommended strategy is to write the harasser a letter, with exact dates and places for everything that's happened (keeping a diary of events can be useful if it comes to a confrontation). Say how you feel about it, and what you want to happen. Keep a copy in case you need to take matters further.

It may be that the harassment is so severe that none of these techniques is sufficient. If things are really bad, recruit allies. Many harassers will clock up more than one victim. Try to find out who the other victims are, band together and complain to your union and to your employing organization. Increasingly unions are taking up the issue of sexual harassment, and even if you can't locate other victims your union should help you to make your complaint. (For detailed practical advice for both women and men read Part Five of Sue Read's book *Sexual Harassment at Work*.)

In the long term, the best hope of finally putting a stop to the phenomenon of sexual harassment at work (apart from a major alteration in the relationship between the sexes, of course . . .) probably lies in a general increase in awareness of the problem. Until recent years, victims didn't even have a name for the humiliating misery they were suffering. Nowadays it is no longer a question of either putting up with it or losing your job. There *are* things that can be done, and action is better than letting things ride.

The milder harassers – the touching, leering, derogatory and 'aren't-you-flattered-by-my-attentions' types of men – might come to realize that their victims hate it but are afraid to say so.

As for the serious harassers, if they can be exposed as men who are unable to deal with women in any but sexual terms, and who are unable to face them as possible competitors at work – well, they're not going to like that image much, are they?[54]

OFFICE AFFAIRS

Now and then, of course, sexual approaches by A are welcomed by B – and lo, we have the full-blown Office Affair.

Surprisingly little research has been done on romance at work, but what there is implies that a) there's quite a lot of it about and b) more often than not it causes trouble.

One British study, for example, sampled senior and middle executives and personnel managers, most of whom were on a masters degree course at Strathclyde Business School. The seventy-six respondents said that in the course of their recent careers they had observed a total of 438 affairs – about six each. The researchers, Ron Harrison and Roger Lee, comment: 'Most respondents were still at an early stage of their careers, so it appears that the incidence of romantic entanglements may be more widespread than some had believed.'[55]

This is perhaps hardly surprising. After all, if you haven't married your childhood or college sweetheart or met Mr/Ms Right at, say, a party, then work will surely be a prime meeting-ground. Working with someone in an organization can bring you together frequently, and proximity, as psychologists have shown, is a strong factor in breeding attraction.[56] And, by definition, you already have a fair amount in common.

The first empirical study of office romances was done by Robert Quinn, an assistant professor in the public administration department at the State University of New York at Albany.[57] Having read about a psychological study in which visitors to Boston airport were found to be a lot more forthcoming than native Bostonians, and having had a lot of difficulty getting anyone to answer his questions about affairs in the office, he approached people waiting at Albany and La Guardia airports and asked them about office affairs they had witnessed.

Types of affair. From his data, Quinn deduced that there were three main types of office affair, at least as perceived by fellow workers:

1. *The fling.* 'The fling is usually characterized by high excitement on the part of both participants and is often accompanied by the belief that the relationship is going to be temporary in duration.'

2. *True love.* 'True love reflects sincerity on the part of both participants. It usually, but not always, involves two unmarried people and tends to end in marriage.'

3. *The utilitarian relationship.* 'The utilitarian relationship is one in which the male is perceived as seeking such things as excitement, ego satisfaction, adventure, and sexual experience, while the female is viewed as in search of organizational rewards.'

Secrecy. Quinn notes that about two thirds of the participants try at first to keep the affair a secret, but they often fail:

> Most work groups are especially sensitive to even minor changes in behavior of their coworkers ... Among the most common activities that alert members of the organization are being observed together away from work, longer or more frequent chats, long lunches together, long discussions behind closed doors, and joint business trips. Less subtle, but surprisingly common tip-offs involve the physical expression of affection. In about a third of the cases, participants are seen embracing in closets, kissing in supply rooms, or fondling in the parking lot.

Dear me.

Effects on the lovers. Sometimes one or both participants changed for the better, perhaps working harder or becoming easier to get on with. But more frequently they lost the respect of the members of their work group, becoming preoccupied and less competent and hard-working. Sometimes, particularly if the romance was between a superior and a subordinate, power manipulations would start up:

> For the male in a higher position than the female, such changes involve showing favoritism to the female, ignoring complaints about her performance, promoting or giving a raise to the female, formally or informally increasing her power, and being inaccessible. For the female, favoritism, the assumption of power, isolating the male, and the flaunting of power are especially prominent.

As an example:

> A corporation president hired an attractive and competent young secretary. After they became romantically involved, he began to delegate tasks that he normally disposed of himself to his secretary. Anxious to accomplish this work, she began to demand necessary kinds of information from vice presidents. Resenting demands and instructions from a secretary, the vice presidents openly resisted her efforts. They soon found, however, that it was more difficult to get access to their boss. The secretary delayed or blocked appointments, calls, and memos. She also became an extended set of eyes and ears for the boss by reporting comments and actions that normally would not have reached him.

Effects on colleagues. The above example illustrates precisely what can happen – a breakdown in the normal channels of communication, as well as hostility and resentment. The more the affair causes distortions of power and competence, the worse colleagues are going to react.

At best, colleagues are simply going to gossip about it and may either actively approve or simply not mind. At worst, Quinn says, they may complain to superiors or even resort to sabotaging the lovers' work.

Although researchers don't offer advice to those involved in an office affair, the most obvious course of action if you are seems to be to take scrupulous care about not letting your own work suffer – which can cause trouble for colleagues – and to avoid favouritism and power plays that will be seen unfairly to benefit you or your lover.

One couple I know, who were unmarried, equal-status colleagues in the same department, fell very much in love. They proceeded to handle the situation extremely well. They kept their affair completely quiet at first – avoiding all those long lunches and lingering looks – and, when they realized it was really serious, announced it to their work-mates and discussed the situation with them.

The couple were anxious to make it clear that they wouldn't let their relationship impinge on their colleagues, and they hoped they didn't mind. Most reacted well to this – but there were still snide comments from one or two; the organization was one that frowned heavily on work-place involvements, and eventually one (the man) left for another post. They are now married.

It can, of course, impose extra strains on colleagues if one or both of the lovers is already married. They might have to answer phone calls from the spouse, or meet him or her at office functions, and generally be let in for a deceitful and embarrassing time.

What to do? At bottom, the research seems to suggest what might be seen as very unpalatable conclusions. If it's a short-term fling, it may be too brief to do much damage at the time to relationships and power balances in the office. But there may, of course, be unpleasant after-effects if it ends badly. So that's a risk.

If the relationship is utilitarian it may well be especially prone to all the most serious problems that can arise – particularly power manipulations. The trouble caused will probably outweigh any benefits.

If it really is love – well. What little research there is implies that it may be better for one to leave or to move to some more distant point in the organization. Otherwise, although all the world loves a lover, they don't love them quite so much right there in the office.

3

Subordinates – how to motivate them

I just can't get Susan to do anything. Well, she'll do the minimum, but that's it. Come 5.30, there's just a blur streaking past – and that's her.

Dick's being a bit funny with me lately. He did a really good piece of work for me – just as I expected – but since then, he's not really been all that friendly. And he never volunteered for that extra job last Saturday afternoon, as he usually would. D'you think I've done something?

Jane's really terrific. She does her job brilliantly, no fuss, never lets me down. We get on well, too – I feel very fortunate.

Most people who work in an office have at least one person working underneath them – the exceptions are nearly always secretaries, a frequently downtrodden group whom I will return to later – and many have more than one. Anyone in this position knows how delicate relationships can be with people below you in the hierarchy. But if you don't manage them well, your own work, your department's work and your reputation can be greatly damaged.

Psychologists have been researching the 'what makes an effective leader?' question for years. (They use the word 'leader' as a general term to mean anyone with influence and power over others.) To be perfectly frank, they're a long way off any really satisfactory answer. The more they look into it, the more complex the whole problem appears.[1] However, a number of themes seem to be emerging:

COMMUNICATION

Or, as Robert Baron puts it, 'cultivate your sensitivity quotient'.[2] It's no good thinking that all you need to do is to behave as you think bosses *ought* to behave – tell your underlings what to do every five minutes, be aloof, or whatever. On the contrary, the evidence is that successful leaders are often highly skilled at understanding their subordinates' needs and adapting their own behaviour and strategies to them.

So how are you to do that?

Start tuning in. You don't have a snowflake in hell's chance of finding out what makes your subordinates tick if you don't talk to them. Simple as this is, a remarkable number of people don't do it.

After all, what do you *really* know about your secretary? Your assistant? The individual members of your department? How often have you heard people say things like: 'It came as such a *shock*. I'd no idea she was unhappy here. But she just walked in this morning, said she couldn't stand it any more and flung down her letter of resignation'?

I'm not suggesting that you should be armed with detailed information on their lives over the past ten years, whether they prefer tangerine to magenta as a car colour, or are allergic to squid. I'm talking about things like their needs, ambitions and aspirations, whether they would like more control over their own work, more participation in decisions, more information, or a clearer idea of what you expect of them.

This 'tuning in to your subordinates' needs' idea is relatively new. Psychologists used to look on a leader's subordinates as though they were all the same. The leader would do X, and they'd all set fire to their in-trays and rush round to the nearest employment agency; the chief would do Y, and productivity would rise by 150 per cent.

But then George Graen, a psychologist from the University

of Cincinnati, and his colleagues suggested that it might be more helpful to look at the relationships leaders had with each of their subordinates *individually*.[3] When you do that, you find that the quality of the relationships can vary considerably: it's not true that you're inevitably 'a divine boss' or 'the pits' with all your subordinates.

Since the quality of these relationships is linked with subordinates' productivity and satisfaction, and with how likely they are to leave the job – 'employee turnover', as they call it in the trade – how good those relationships are matters a lot. Bosses with high turnover may be looked at a bit askance by *their* bosses: 'Simkins has lost half the graphics department since he took over as head. What in God's name is he doing?'

A demonstration. Locking into your subordinates as individuals really can work. George Graen, with his colleague Terri Scandura, tried out the practical implications of their approach with members of an entire department in a large government installation in the Midwest.

What they did was to train intensively the managers of some of the work units, and not the remainder, so they could later assess the results of their training. The idea was to encourage the managers to do four things:

1. The managers were to spend time asking about and discussing each person's gripes, concerns and expectations about their job, their supervisor's job and their working relationship.

2. Using 'active listening' skills learned in the training, the managers were to be particularly attentive and sensitive to what issues were raised and how they were formulated by each subordinate.

3. The managers were to refrain from imposing their own frame of reference about the issues raised.

4. The managers were to share some of their expectations

about their own job, their subordinate's job and their working relationship.[4]

The term 'active listening' means you should, as Robert Baron puts it, 'Ask questions, occasionally try to put the speaker's comments in your own words. Such steps will help you stay alert, and will facilitate your processing of the information presented.'[5] In other words, don't just sit there nodding glassily like those stuffed dogs people put in the back windows of their cars.

After their training the managers spent thirty to forty minutes having a private talk with each of their subordinates along these lines.

The researchers already knew how good the relationships were between these managers and each of their subordinates. At the beginning of the study the subordinates had been asked to tick one of four answers (in italics below, with the score for each answer in brackets) to each of the following questions about their boss:

1. Do you usually feel that you know where you stand . . . do you usually know how satisfied your immediate supervisor is with what you do? *Always know where I stand* (4); *Usually know where I stand* (3); *Seldom know where I stand* (2); *Never know where I stand* (1)

2. How well do you feel that your immediate supervisor understands your problems and needs? *Completely* (4); *Well enough* (3); *Some but not enough* (2); *Not at all* (1)

3. How well do you feel that your immediate supervisor recognizes your potential? *Fully* (4); *As much as the next person* (3); *Some but not enough* (2); *Not at all* (1)

4. Regardless of how much formal authority your immediate supervisor has built into his or her position, what are the chances that he or she would be personally inclined to use power to help you solve problems in your work? *Certainly would* (4); *Probably would* (3); *Might or might not* (2); *No chance* (1)

5. Again, regardless of the amount of formal authority your immediate supervisor has, to what extent can you count on him or her to 'bail you out' at his or her expense when you really need it? *Certainly would* (4); *Probably would* (3); *Might or might not* (2); *No chance* (1)

6. I have enough confidence in my immediate supervisor that I would defend and justify his or her decisions if he or she were not present to do so. *Certainly would* (4); *Probably would* (3); *Maybe* (2); *Probably not* (1)

7. How would you characterize your working relationship with your immediate supervisor? *Extremely effective* (4); *Better than average* (3); *About average* (2); *Less than average* (1)

The scores were then added up for each participant. (Why not try it, imagining what your subordinates would say? If you think any of them would give you a total of no more than seven, you'd better do something quickly ... But, of course, the worst thing is that you might *not know*.)

What Scandura and Graen found was that, in the three months following the training, compared to the subordinates whose managers had not received it, those with initially poor relationships with their bosses showed significant gains. Their productivity improved; they were more satisfied with their job and with their boss; they felt more willing to take on additional responsibility; and they thought their boss was more supportive.

The subordinates who had initially poor quality relationships with their supervisor were not, the researchers say, necessarily the poor performers in the work units before the experiment. They 'clearly had the *potential* to consistently produce at higher levels, but it appears that they did not perceive higher performance as being worth the effort'.

'As a practical matter,' the researchers conclude modestly, 'the leadership intervention produced a 19% improvement in hard productivity. This improvement resulted in an estimated annual cost saving of over $5 million.'[6]

Heady stuff. But most of us would be happy with a generally better working relationship with our subordinates even if they might not produce quite such spectacular results.

PEOPLE AND PRODUCTIVITY

One reason why George Graen and his colleagues' ideas are so attractive is that they show clearly how leaders can combine concern for their subordinates as people with concern for productivity. After all, if you're so sweet and considerate to your subordinates that you never like to bother them to do nasty things like meet deadlines or produce high-quality work on difficult projects, *they* may love you but your superiors won't.

Again, if you stride into their office clad (metaphorically speaking) in black, steel-studded leather, fiercely demand that report right *now*, you lazy bastards, and you don't care if Kevin's dog has just got run over, they'll undoubtedly produce as required. But you'll probably be deafened by the rustling of newspapers as they all search the sits. vac. pages for another job.

As Robert Baron puts it:

> Is it necessary to choose between good relations with one's subordinates and a high level of productivity? At one time, many managers believed that this was true: one could either be liked, *or* get the job done. Recent evidence indicates that this is simply not true. In fact, leaders who combine these two orientations – who demonstrate their concern with both people and production – tend to get the best of both worlds. When you serve as a leader, then, try to adopt this double-sided approach. The chances are quite good that your results will be better than if you choose to focus on only one or the other of these contrasting approaches.[7]

However, the reason Robert Baron uses careful phrases like 'the chances are quite good' is that in some circumstances a greater concentration on either people *or* productivity may be appropriate. Psychologists are still struggling to find out exactly what those circumstances are.[8]

It may be, for example, that in times of acute crisis it would be better to focus strongly on getting the job done. Or, if the people who work for you are highly competent and motivated, it may be better to concentrate on good relationships. Such subordinates might become extremely resentful if you 'keep interfering' rather than letting them get on with the job. 'I swear, if he tells me one more time that Harrods is the best retail outlet for our sapphire-encrusted lavatory roll holders, I'm going to bean him with one.'

Some subordinates, however, might want more guidance and monitoring than others; if you talk to them in the way Terri Scandura and George Graen suggested, you'll know which they are.

How much participation?

This is a really tricky question for people who have others working under them – how much should you let them participate in running the show? Some leaders simply shut themselves in their offices, make the decisions, fling open the door and announce to their subordinates what's going to happen. 'OK. We're going to dump the Kittyfood account, recruit an assistant creative director, work on Saturdays for the next eight weeks on that Tory party job, and move the offices to a converted warehouse in Hackney.'

Others – probably a much rarer breed – won't even authorize the purchase of a new kettle without calling a departmental meeting first.

So what's the best plan?

Research findings have not been all that clear-cut. But, roughly speaking, letting subordinates participate tends to make them more satisfied with their jobs, but does not necessarily increase productivity.[9]

It *may* do so if, say, participation results in the group setting high or difficult goals. And having more people involved in a decision can improve its quality.

But when should you ask them to participate? For what sorts of decisions? Two psychologists, Victor Vroom and Philip Yetton, have come up with a precise model to help you decide, one which has research evidence to support it.[10]

You're going to have to hang on to your hats a bit for this one. But although it *sounds* complicated, Philip Yetton says: 'With over 5,000 managers in the U.S.A., Europe and Australia trained in the original model, few have complained that it is too complex.'[11]

Vroom and Yetton suggest, first of all, that there are five main ways a leader can make a decision about a problem. In the list below, A means an autocratic process, C a consultative process and G group decision-making:

LEVELS OF PARTICIPATION

A1 You solve the problem or make the decision yourself using the information available to you at the present time.

A2 You obtain any necessary information from subordinates, then decide on a solution to the problem yourself. You may or may not tell subordinates the purpose of your questions or give information about the problem or decision you are working on. The input provided by them is clearly in response to your request for specific information. They do *not* play a role in the definition of the problem or in generating or evaluating alternative solutions.

C1 You share the problem with the relevant subordinates individually, getting their ideas and suggestions without bringing them together as a group. Then *you* make the decision. This decision may or may not reflect your subordinates' influence.

C2 You share the problem with your subordinates in a group meeting. In this meeting you obtain their ideas and suggestions. Then *you* make the decision, which may or may not reflect your subordinates' input.

G You share the problem with your subordinates as a group. Together you generate and evaluate alternatives and attempt to reach agreement (consensus) on a solution. Your role is much like that of chairperson. You coordinate the discussion, keep it focused on the problem, and make sure that the critical issues are discussed. You can provide the group with information or ideas that you have, but do not try to 'press' them to adopt 'your' solution; and you are willing to accept and implement any solution that has the support of the entire group.[12]

Which of these five 'levels of participation' should you choose for any particular problem? The Vroom–Yetton model suggests seven rules to follow. The idea is to go through the rules one by one, eliminating any style that is 'not feasible' given the prevailing circumstances. You should then be left with one or more actions which Vroom and Yetton say are within the 'feasible set' of possible options. The seven rules are:

RULES TO PROTECT THE QUALITY OF THE DECISION

1. THE LEADER INFORMATION RULE.
   If the quality of the decision is important and the leader does not possess enough information or expertise to solve the problem by him or herself, then cross off A1.

2. THE GOAL CONGRUENCE RULE.

If the quality of the decision is important and subordinates are *not* likely to pursue the organization's goals in their efforts to solve this problem, then cross off G.

3. THE UNSTRUCTURED PROBLEM RULE.

In decisions where the quality of the decision is important, the leader lacks the necessary information or expertise to solve the problem by her or himself, and the problem is unstructured, you will need the subordinates likely to possess relevant information to be involved *together* in solving the problem. So cross off A1, A2 and C1.

RULES TO PROTECT THE ACCEPTANCE OF THE DECISION

4. THE ACCEPTANCE RULE.

If the acceptance of the decision by subordinates is critical to whether or not it will be implemented effectively, and if it is not certain that an autocratic decision will be accepted, then cross off A1 and A2.

5. THE CONFLICT RULE.

If acceptance of the decision is critical, an autocratic decision is not certain to be accepted and disagreement among subordinates in methods of attaining the organizational goal is likely, then those in disagreement need to be able to talk through and resolve their differences with full knowledge of the problem. So cross off A1, A2 and C1, which don't permit any discussion among subordinates.

6. THE FAIRNESS RULE.

If the quality of the decision is unimportant, but acceptance of the decision is critical and not certain to result from an autocratic decision, then subordinates need to interact with one another and negotiate over the fair method of resolving any differences. They should have full responsibility for determining what is fair and equitable. So cross off A1, A2, C1 and C2.

7. THE ACCEPTANCE PRIORITY RULE

If acceptance is critical, not certain to result from an autocratic decision, and if subordinates are motivated to pursue the organizational goals represented in the problem, then equal partnership in the decision-making process can produce greater acceptance without risking the quality of the decision. So cross off A1, A2, C1 and C2.[13]

The decision methods left standing after you've been through the seven rules are the ones in the 'feasible set'.

An example. Although the above might look over-complicated, it really is quite easy to use. Suppose, for example, that one of your department's most valuable clients has suddenly started giving a lot of trouble – complaining about the prices you're charging, changing their minds about using an Arabian sheik in a publicity stunt at the very moment when he is landing at Heathrow airport with a bevy of supertough henchmen, that kind of thing.

The whole department is involved with this particular client, and individuals are bound to possess details of their various dealings that you do not have. Vital nuggets of information could have been dropped after the second bottle of wine when James and Sally took their client organization's MD to the Ritz last Wednesday . . .

So what's to be done?

Well, as the decision is important and you don't possess all the available information (see rule 1), you shouldn't make the decision by yourself based only on the information you have; so cross A1 off the list.

Your subordinates, don't forget, are currently feeling a bit cheesed off with your organization because it was jolly mean with the last pay rise. So, following rule 2, it's probably best to forget G.

The problem about what to do with this client is extremely open-ended and 'unstructured'. Do you withdraw your services? Get your own boss to take their MD out for a day on the golf links to try to get to the bottom of it? Unleash the Arab sheik's henchmen on to them? Or what? So, as rule 3 suggests, you can knock off A2 and C1 (you've already eliminated A1).

Following through the remaining rules, you'll see that for this particular problem no more options have to be eliminated. Nor can they be: in this particular case, there is only one option left – C2, calling a group meeting, listening to their views, taking a deep breath and then taking the decision yourself.

Of course, in some circumstances you'll find that once you've gone through the seven rules there are still several options left in the 'feasible set'. But the best option will probably be fairly clear to you at the time; for example, it may be necessary to choose the alternative that's going to take the least time because everything's at panic stations.

It is advisable to bear in mind one further point. As Robert Baron points out: 'In general, subordinates prefer a participative approach. Thus, if you must err, do so in this direction. The costs will probably be small relative to those incurred by a leadership style subordinates find too autocratic.'[14]

Setting goals

Talking of participation raises the question of whether or not you can best motivate your subordinates by involving them in setting their own work goals.

Psychologists have done a lot of research on goal-setting and performance, and the evidence is that it's better for your subordinates to have specific, difficult goals to work towards than it is just to give them general goals, to tell them to 'do their best' or to give them no goals at all.[15]

Given goals of equal difficulty, there is some (but not yet conclusive) evidence that it is slightly better if your subordinates have taken part in setting them than if you have imposed them.[16]

But this may be difficult to arrange. Say you are making a pitch for a contract to mount a special exhibition at London Zoo. Your subordinates may suggest that they try to have a draft plan for the exhibition, based around a collection of pictures and models of wild animals, ready in four weeks' time. You, on the other hand, might want them to have a full plan, incorporating details of how to obtain live tigers and at least one rare monkey from the upper reaches of the Amazon, ready by next Monday.

The best thing might be to go for a Vroom–Yetton-style 'consultative' procedure, making sure you incorporate their views as far as possible in the light of whatever pressure there might be from outside or the powers-that-be above you. You might well, for example, not have appreciated precisely what is or is not feasible from your more elevated vantage-point.

Ideally the goal should be specific and challenging, and yet your subordinates should feel that they played at least some part in deciding what it was to be. One reason why it is better to settle on a specific goal rather than to adopt a more general 'do your best' policy is that specific goals lead people to plan and organize more than they otherwise would.[17]

Rewards

So here they are, beavering away for you. What sort of things do you say to them after the job's done? 'Well *done*, a really excellent piece of work'? 'Mmmhm ngh'? Nothing at all? 'That was the *worst*. A demented crayfish could have done better'?

It's generally advisable to say *something* rather than nothing; giving subordinates feedback on their performance is widely regarded as being a good idea.[18] *Informative* comments on what people have done are always useful. 'I think if you'd made the conclusion a bit punchier ...' And the evidence is that rewards are more effective than punishments, as long as they are given for a particular piece of work or event ('contingent') rather than being handed out indiscriminately ('noncontingent').

Philip Podsakoff of Indiana University and his colleagues have looked at the punish/reward issue. They gave questionnaires to nearly 2000 employees from three different organizations: local government workers, hospital pharmacists and state government employees.

One of the questionnaires asked people to say how their bosses treated them in terms of reward or punishment. Each item was in the form of a statement, and participants had to say how true it was of their supervisor. The questionnaire was divided into four sections (although this would not have been obvious to the respondents), like this:

CONTINGENT REWARD BEHAVIOUR

1. My supervisor always gives me positive feedback when I perform well.

2. My supervisor gives me special recognition when my work performance is especially good.

3. My supervisor would quickly acknowledge an improvement in the quality of my work.

4. My supervisor commends me when I do a better than average job.

5. My supervisor personally pays me a compliment when I do outstanding work.

6. My supervisor informs his/her boss and/or others in the organization when I do outstanding work.

7. If I do well my supervisor will reward me.

8. My supervisor would do all that (s)he could to help me go as far as I would like to go in this organization if my work was consistently above average.

9. My good performance often goes unacknowledged by my supervisor.

10. I often perform well in my job and still receive no praise from my supervisor.

CONTINGENT PUNISHMENT BEHAVIOUR

11. If I performed at a level below that which I was capable of, my supervisor would indicate his/her disapproval.

12. My supervisor shows his/her displeasure when my work is below acceptable standards.

13. My supervisor lets me know about it when I perform poorly.

14. My supervisor would reprimand me if my work was below standard.

15. When my work is not up to par, my supervisor points it out to me.

NONCONTINGENT PUNISHMENT BEHAVIOUR

16. My supervisor frequently holds me accountable for things I have no control over.

17. My supervisor is often displeased with my work for no apparent reason.

18. My supervisor is often critical of my work even when I perform well.

19. I frequently am reprimanded by my supervisor without knowing why.

NONCONTINGENT REWARD BEHAVIOUR

20. Even when I perform poorly, my supervisor often commends me.

21. My supervisor is just as likely to praise me when I do poorly as when I do well.

22. Even when I perform poorly on my job, my supervisor rarely gets upset with me.

23. My supervisor frequently praises me even when I don't deserve it.[19]

What Podsakoff and his colleagues found was that 'contingent reward behaviour' appeared to be the most effective strategy. It was linked not only with higher performance but with all their five measures of job satisfaction: that is, subordinates' satisfaction with their work, supervisor, co-workers, pay and opportunities for advancement in the job.

'Noncontingent reward behaviour' and 'contingent punishment behaviour', however, bore little relation either to subordinates' performance or to their job satisfaction. Praising apparently at random or punishment of poor performance didn't seem to do any good at all – or too much harm, for that matter.

But 'noncontingent punishment' seemed pretty fatal. It was related not only to lowered performance on the job but also to employees' dissatisfaction, particularly with their supervisor, co-workers and pay.

Work sampling

For rewards to be effective, then, they have to be contingent on what your employees have actually done. But do you usually know what they *are* doing? Does the fact that Martin is scrawling over sheet after sheet of paper mean that he's finally had a creative breakthrough about how to stop the chimps at London Zoo doing offputting things at peak infant-school visiting times, or that he's writing to his girlfriend to find out what she was doing at the Limelight last night with that greaseball in the gold lamé boiler suit?

You will know what some of your subordinates are up to,

of course, if you work very closely with them – but what about the rest?

An American psychologist, Judith Komaki, has done a relatively rare type of study – of what effective and ineffective managers *actually do*. She analysed the behaviour of twenty-four managers in two divisions of a large Midwestern medical insurance firm. 'Managers in the two divisions,' she says, 'were primarily concerned with the processing of claims and correspondence and the reviewing of medical records; managers in select departments dealt with audits, reimbursements, and sales.'

Half the managers she looked at had been ranked by their superiors in the top quarter of all the organization's managers in terms of motivating others; the other half were in the bottom quarter. Trained observers scrutinized each manager up to twenty times, for half an hour at a time, over a seven-month period.

The results revealed only one difference between the effective and 'marginal' managers in terms of their work practices. That is, that the effective ones monitored their employees' work significantly more frequently than did the others.

'The effective managers spent on average 2.9% of their time monitoring performance, whereas the marginal managers spent 2.0%,' Judith Komaki says. 'Although the absolute difference was not large, relatively speaking, almost 50% more time was spent monitoring performance by the effective managers.'

More specifically, the effective managers more often used a particular method of monitoring – work sampling. 'Instead of relying on self-reports or secondary sources, they observed employees (e.g., watched employees processing claims, listened to employees talking with clients on the phone) and inspected the products of their work (e.g., examined computer printouts, processed claims). Especially compelling was the fact that 11 of 12 of the effective managers sampled the work, whereas only 4 of the 12 marginal managers ever once did.'[20]

Although Komaki doesn't point this out, it would probably be as well to do the monitoring fairly inconspicuously. There is evidence that one of the things employees dislike is having a supervisor who 'watches over your shoulder while you are working'.[21]

Komaki found no difference between the effective and ineffective managers in how much time they spent asking subordinates *directly* about their work ('How's the job going?' 'Are we all ready for Wednesday's meeting as far as you know?'), or getting information about their performance from someone else ('What is Dan working on?' 'Did Jim get back with you like he was supposed to?'). Nor were there any differences in how much time they spent making positive, neutral or negative comments on their subordinates' performance, thus indicating awareness of what they had done ('I noticed you showed the 1008 in your report.' 'You saved us from making a very big mistake.').

Why should work sampling be so important, then? Komaki thinks that it enables managers 'to obtain fair and accurate information'. The advantage of this is that, although effective managers don't make *more* comments (which Komaki refers to as 'providing consequences') to their subordinates, 'they may be more likely to provide *contingent* consequences'.[22] In other words, they will be more prone to reward people when they deserve it, as Podsakoff and his colleagues' research recommends.

The poor-performing subordinate

But what are you to do if Barry's minutes of important committee meetings always look as if he were asleep during the crucial bits, or if Jessica's last report looked as though it had been typed by an uncoordinated octopus in the last stages of nervous exhaustion?

Why are they doing badly? The first thing, of course, is to try to work out the reason why your subordinate's performance is not up to scratch. Lack of ability? Lack of motivation? Drink? Personal crisis? Too much pressure? A too difficult task?

The trouble with this is that people are prone to biases in judging the causes of others' behaviour – as in the 'fundamental attribution error' described on p. 35. But another kind of bias is called the 'actor-observer' error. That is, we tend to cite 'external' causes for our own behaviour – pressure, crisis, a difficult task, other aspects of our situation – and 'internal' causes for others' behaviour. For example, they're lazy, disorganized, not clever enough, or whatever.[23]

Therefore while you will tend to downplay the external causes of your subordinates' performance, they will give those causes major weight. It's important to be aware of these biases, as your judgement of the causes will influence what you decide to do about the problem – whether to try to change (or even replace) the person, or to adjust the work setting. Leaders who attribute a subordinate's poor performance to internal causes tend to respond more punitively, and are particularly damning if they believe it is due to lack of effort rather than lack of ability.[24]

You may also find yourself blaming the person rather than the situation because it's easier that way. According to the American psychologist and management expert Terence Mitchell, 'It seems as if supervisors are less likely to look at and understand ways that a task can be changed. We are much more apt to simply try to change the person rather than the task. This bias is partly caused by the fact that it is somehow easier to tell someone to "be different" than to try to change the environment.'[25] If the problem was really, say, that your subordinate simply has too much work to do, it may be that you can do little about that because you're too under-staffed.

What to do? It is possible to change the way you assess your subordinates' performance. In one study students were shown a video of a woman working as an editorial assistant and falling very badly behind with her work.

One group of students were told that there were certain important factors in the situation: 'frequent incoming telephone calls and interruptions from people, unexpected additional work, other people not meeting their deadlines, unreasonable time pressures, and her supervisor's shifting expectations about her duties'.

Others were told that there were various 'internal' causes, such as poor organizational skills and social talking during a busy period. The remaining students were not told anything about the possible causes of her bad performance.

The results showed that, compared to the other two groups, those students who'd had her situation pointed out to them made more 'external' attributions for her performance.[26] So you can sensitize yourself to these possibilities.

If you feel that something in your subordinate's personal or work circumstances was indeed responsible for their poor performance, then not only will punishment or threats almost certainly do no good, but you need to talk to him or her about what the problem might be and how – if it's possible – you can help them with it. But if, trying to remember your natural biases, you still think that the cause of their poor work is down to them personally, then what should you do?

We have already seen that punishment is not the best idea. Instead, what you have to do is to make it clear what they have done that falls short of your expectations and what is required, but in a constructive way. In his major review of research on leadership, Alan Bryman of Loughborough University argues that the 'one minute reprimand' is highly compatible with the idea of 'contingent reward'.[27]

The one minute reprimand. The one minute reprimand comes from a book called *The One Minute Manager* by Kenneth

Blanchard and Spencer Johnson, based on the authors' management and medical experiences.[28] Psychologically it makes a great deal of sense.

The idea, as Bryman describes it, is as follows:

> The 'one minute reprimand' . . . is really a positive response to a disappointing performance. The manager lets the subordinate know in clear terms as quickly as possible what is wrong and how he or she feels about it. But the manager also reassures the subordinate, reaffirms how much that person is valued and how much is thought of them in spite of the poor performance. Further, when the reprimand ends, it is not carried over into other situations . . . On the face of it, the one-minute reprimand is a form of contingent punishment behaviour. In fact, the brevity of the reprimand, coupled with the reassurance that the subordinate receives, seem to make it a sub-type of positive reward behaviour.

Blanchard and Johnson's work, Bryman believes, 'suggests that an emphasis on making the individual feel good, even when having to be reprimanded for a disappointing performance, is a better platform for the management of subordinate performance than a punitive strategy'.[29]

Making people feel good. As I mentioned in the last chapter, the importance of realizing that people need to feel good about themselves cannot be over-emphasized. If you can bear that in mind in your dealings with your subordinates you will make both your and their working lives a great deal more effective and pleasant. Although I'm not a great believer in 'golden rules' – life is a bit *too* complicated for that – this would be my nomination.

Secretaries

Secretarial work provides a classic illustration of an arena where this 'rule' should be applied a great deal more than it is. If you are a secretary you may already be nodding vigorously. If you're not, the chances are that even if you don't have a number of people working underneath you, you will at least have access to a secretary – sometimes shared, sometimes working for you exclusively.

Secretaries, unsurprisingly, do not like being treated as dogsbodies;[30] and yet they frequently are. A professional woman friend of mine told me what happens at lunchtimes when the secretaries are out and calls are put straight through. 'It's a salutary experience hearing how secretaries are spoken to as opposed to someone they know is a high status colleague. People can be very rude, and they get cross and take it out on the secretaries.' I, too, have answered the phone when our secretary was out, and when people hear a woman's voice they often assume I am she. It's remarkable how the supercilious, patronizing tone changes when they discover I'm not.

I have also often noticed how colleagues treat their secretaries in a brusque and patronizing way, as though they were typing machines with legs. It not only makes the secretaries feel miserable and resentful but my colleagues usually suffer for it in the end, too.

Secretaries who feel badly treated, no matter how much they take pride in their work, are simply not going to be as likely to put themselves out for someone who does not treat them as a person. What's more, secretaries are far from being powerless: they influence your image to outsiders. Many's the time I've rung someone in another organization at 3.45 p.m. and been told blithely, 'Oh, I'm afraid she's still at lunch.' Or 'Mr Jones? Well, I'm sorry, we never know *where* he is.' They also know a great deal of office gossip, and frequently have your boss's ear too.

So if you have contact with secretaries, my advice is simply to recognize that they are people, with skills that you need, who want to value themselves and their work just as you do

– and everything should follow from that. For example, why not tell them what that report you've just asked them to type is about? Who it's for? How it fits into the scheme of things? Why it's urgent?

If you are a secretary yourself and you feel insufficiently valued, the best plan is probably to try to break the 'typing machine with legs' kind of stereotype. Offer to do things that lie outside your assigned duties: if you arrange meetings when you were hired as a glorified typist, say, your boss will have to shift his or her view of you. As you become more relied on, you should become more valued – and then is the time to ask for a pay rise to confirm it. If you don't ask for some form of recognition, it's often a short step from being relied on and valued to relied on and exploited.

WOMEN BOSSES

If you're a woman in a position of leadership, you may have problems of another type: a fear that you will not be seen as a competent boss worthy of respect. That women are discriminated against in the work-place generally is not in doubt – you have only to look at the struggle women have to climb the ladder in nearly all the professions.

The crumb of comfort I can offer is that increasingly, both sexes are seeing male and female bosses similarly, rather than rating men more highly.[31] This does not mean there isn't a long way to go. For example, a study published in 1982 found that men and women who were participative in their leadership styles were rated equally favourably, but while male autocratic leaders were given modest positive ratings, autocratic women were definitely rated negatively. In other words, women leaders weren't allowed to 'get away with it' to the same extent as men (you'll remember that people generally prefer participative leadership anyway).[32]

But there are signs of a shift towards less sexism at work.

And if you treat your subordinates in the ways I have described, you will, let us devoutly hope, find them happy to work with you.

The particular problems of being a woman in an office environment will keep surfacing throughout this book; if you want to read in more depth on this subject try Rosabeth Moss Kanter's *Men and Women of the Corporation*, Cary Cooper and Marilyn Davidson's *High Pressure: working lives of women managers* and Janice LaRouche and Regina Ryan's *Strategies for Women at Work*.[33]

FAIRNESS AND COMPETENCE

How you behave as a boss will be a vital component of your subordinates' satisfaction with their jobs. Robert Baron says:

> When employees approve of the style adopted by their supervisors, perceive these persons as fair, and believe they have the ability to help them with their jobs or within the organization generally, satisfaction tends to be high. When, in contrast, they dislike their supervisors' approach to management, view them as incompetent, or believe they have little influence within the organization, satisfaction tends to be low.[34]

Psychologists have found, surprisingly, that subordinates' performance is not very strongly linked to how satisfied they are with the job.[35] But job satisfaction can have myriad subtle effects that straight measures of performance might not always capture – such as being helpful to colleagues, showing greater sensitivity to others and, of course, not hot-footing it to the nearest employment agency.[36]

And, let's face it, who wouldn't rather be surrounded by a pleasant, cooperative atmosphere than a miasma of misery, resentment and hostility . . .

Bosses – how to handle them

My boss drives me crazy. *Here I am, good at my job, qualified to the back teeth, and he treats me like a schoolkid. I keep having this recurring dream, that he's an exam invigilator, and I'm sitting at one of those collapsible wooden desks covered with engraved names and inkspots, worrying what he's going to say if I don't answer all these questions in three hours flat.*

I don't know why he keeps snapping at me. I can't do anything right, he complains about the slightest thing, hangs around my desk at two o'clock and scowls at me if I get back from lunch at thirty seconds past. And my desk is constantly covered with an absolute snowstorm of nagging memos from him.

I really like my boss. She listens to what I say, asks my advice, never bawls me out in public. I keep expecting to wake up one day and find she's been replaced by some supercilious bastard like the one I had in my last job.

Bosses. Oh dear oh dear oh dear. Of all the things people find to complain about in their office lives, the iniquities of The Boss do seem to be an endlessly recurring theme. Incompetent, bullying, patronizing, aggressive, back-stabbing, grabbing praise that should have been yours, taking no notice of anything you say, never telling you anything, picking on you, and so on and so on.

The question is, if you have a difficult boss, how should you cope? And if you don't have a difficult boss, how can you get the most out of your relationship? It is curious that although there's simply masses of research literature on how to deal with your subordinates, there is remarkably little on how to deal with your superiors.

But there are things you can do that make psychological sense. Some of the general tactics you may already recognize by now; the importance of understanding what individuals are about and what they want and need, of deducing the causes of their behaviour as accurately as you can, and of realizing that they need to feel good about themselves too.

Find out about them. As with your subordinates, it's vital to try to find out what makes your boss tick. Unfortunately, you can't be as direct as you can with your own subordinates, because in this relationship bosses are the ones with the power. They may not wish to disclose too much information about themselves, as a way of maintaining their higher status over you.[1]

Just imagine how you would react if your boss suddenly put his feet on the desk, leant back and said 'God, I've just got to tell you, I had this *terrific* row with Miranda last night. And she picked up this shell paperweight we bought in Bournemouth last year and dashed it to the ground. I mean, I just didn't know what to do.'

Uncomfortable, don't you think? But why? Essentially, he has stepped too far outside the boss 'role' and is treating you as a status equal. That may be just what you want, and it may come in the end if you establish an extremely friendly relationship with your boss – but such a contingency is unlikely. For bosses to feel that they can exert power and leadership over you, they may need to keep 'in role', in the jargon, and not close the personal gap between you too far.

But still, the more you know about your boss the better, as this can help you to work out why he or she behaves towards you in a particular way, and how you can best get along together. Try to find out what you can, through office gossip (but beware of false leads!) and your own observations.

DIFFICULTIES WITH THE BOSS

The awful-to-everyone boss

Let's take the worst case first: that your boss is simply vile to everybody all the time.

If you gather enough information about him, you may see ways of minimizing his awful behaviour with you. (The sex of your putative boss will vary randomly throughout this chapter – no sexism here, I promise!)

It could be, for example, that he is very insecure. Office gossip may tell you that he's been on the brink of being fired for years and if it weren't for the chairman's daughter . . . Or he got the sack from his last job when his subordinates didn't back him up on a major decision which went wrong . . .

Such insecurity is often, in my experience, the core problem with unnaturally aggressive or authoritarian bosses. If this is the case with your boss, the key is never to threaten him. If you have to disagree with him on some point, say 'You're the boss, of course, but I just wonder if we shouldn't consider . . .' 'You've been right about that firm all along, but it did just occur to me that now they have a new managing director they might be more amenable to our offer . . .'

All bosses need to feel they do a good job – this sort especially. If you can say anything positive or appreciative to him, in a way that doesn't sound false and creepy, then do so. 'I don't know how you got that sales director to back down so quickly.' 'I've put in that extra paragraph you recommended – I think it reads much better now.'

Personal distance. You also need to be a bit careful of your non-verbal behaviour with a status-conscious boss. Psychologists have found that when two people are of different status, they prefer to sit further apart when talking than do people of equal status.[2] So if you approach a status-conscious boss too closely, he may quite literally feel that you're not keeping your respectful distance!

A friend of mine once had a boss whose chair was one of those typists' chairs with castors. He used to shoot backwards, castors squeaking, early on in their conversations, and thereafter ricochet around the room in a thoroughly unnerving manner.

As we know from chapter 2, this sort of behaviour can lead to some unfortunate misunderstandings. As Canadian psychologist Robert Gifford puts it:

> If John perceives himself to be of higher status than Peter, present results suggest that he will prefer a greater interpersonal distance than if he perceives Peter as a peer. But if Peter's reading of the situation is that he and John are of equal status, Peter will be seeking the smaller distance. As Peter approaches, John will feel that 'this nobody' is crowding him and may express his feeling non-verbally. If John consequently begins to increase the existing distance between them, Peter may be hurt because his peer is 'running away' from him and seems to choose to be 'distant'. Both may begin to make attributions: John thinks of Peter as pushy, while Peter wonders if perhaps his mouthwash or deodorant has failed him.[3]

What was happening in my friend's case (the deodorant explanation not being applicable, she hastens to add – after all, no one else behaved like that to her . . .) was that, although perfectly aware that this man was her boss, she didn't see the status difference between them as quite as large as he seemed to. So he kept backing off to re-establish his higher-status distance. If your boss goes into retreat every time you pull up a chair, then you can guess what's happening.

Posture and touch. Psychologists have found that higher-status people tend to lean back and relax much more than their subordinates, who sit more rigidly upright. They also touch those of lower status more frequently than the other way round.[4]

So if you loll back casually during work conversations and uninhibitedly clap him on the back when bumping into him on the way to the canteen, the insecure boss isn't going to like it one little bit.

The awful-to-you boss

It may be, however, that your boss is scratchy with you but not with anyone else. Or that she has become extremely crabby with you only of late, having been fine before. What are the possibilities? Have you personally done something to anger her? Do you get on her nerves? Or does her behaviour have nothing to do with you at all?

Because your boss has power over you, you may be especially prone to bad anxiety attacks when she is out of sorts. 'Oh no, it must be me. She didn't like that last report.' 'I should have remembered never to put Jeremy through to her when she's in an editorial meeting.' 'Or could it have been that time when . . .?'

It may not be your fault. The first thing is, as *The Hitch-Hiker's Guide to the Galaxy* so wisely says, DON'T PANIC. Don't automatically assume you must have done something dreadful. Watch your boss carefully. Is she behaving like this to other people besides yourself? Do the crabby attacks come on particularly after she's been on the phone for an hour with her office door closed? Or after she's just had a meeting with *her* boss?

Your own observations, plus a dose of office gossip, could clarify things greatly. Perhaps her husband has recently announced that he can't stand the sight of her any more and is going to the Andes to meditate and imbibe strange mushrooms. Perhaps she's heard rumours that she's about to be replaced and is busy ringing every ally she possesses in a fever of despair and terror. Perhaps her boss is leaning on her heavily to up her department's productivity or else . . .

Once you have a workable hypothesis, you can take this into account when dealing with her. You can be especially supportive, perhaps, or remember never to burst in on her just after she's been on the phone for an hour or just after her visits to head office.

It's you. OK. Perhaps she's being crabby only with you, and not at times that relate to anything else in her life as far as you can see. What are the main possibilities here?

1. Personality clash.
2. She doesn't like your work.
3. She feels threatened by your competence and success.

Personality clash. Any boss worth his salt will do his best to overlook the fact that he doesn't warm to you personally *if you do your job well*. Try to make sure that your boss realizes you do a good job without being too obvious about it. 'I got hold of Professor Zeppelin yesterday; managed to persuade him to stop off on his way to the Nobel prize-giving ceremony and see us for an hour.' 'Our client really liked the Snoozy report, by the way – she says she'll be in touch with you about it.'

You can also try to minimize your clashes with the boss. When she seems especially irritable with you, think back to what event preceded it, and listen carefully to what she says. For example, if she says, 'Come in, come in. Don't just lurk there, for heaven's sake,' think what you have just been doing. Had you been standing outside her door, shifting from foot to foot, finally poking your head round it in the manner of a diffident tortoise?

Do you *always* do that?

It may be that certain things you do irritate her inordinately, in the same way that perhaps a colleague drives you mad by constantly saying 'If I've said it once I've said it a hundred times,' or whatever little foible you find particularly grating on the nerves.

Once you've worked out what it is, you can then stop doing it. Knock sharply on her door and stride right in.

Is it your work? It may be that, unknown to you, your boss is dissatisfied with the quality or quantity of your work, but finds it difficult to tell you this – or else assumes you know your work isn't good enough but that you don't care or can't do better.

If you suspect this – maybe she has dropped the odd hint – then you need to find out exactly what is wrong. If you have colleagues you can trust, they may have heard something and be able to tell you. Or you could observe their work output and see if yours is radically different, although your work may not be comparable in that way.

But it may be that you simply have to go to your boss and ask outright. 'I feel you have been displeased with my work lately, but I don't know what is wrong, and I would like to put it right.'

This shows that you care about what is happening and that you want to rectify it. Given such an opening, your boss will, let's hope, feel encouraged to tell you explicitly.

Ideally, matters should not reach such a head. When you start a new job or get a new boss, it is probably best to have a discussion early on about precisely what your job entails and what level and type of performance you are expected to produce. Similarly, if you feel you need some feedback from your boss, then ask for it.

Leonard Sandler, a management expert and senior lecturer at Boston University, recounts this wonderful story:

I know a programmer who telephoned a software development manager to ask whether he still had a programming position available. The manager replied that he did have a position available but it had been filled about three months earlier.

The programmer asked, 'Is the person you hired dependable, does he get along well with others, does he show initiative, and write virtually bug-free code?' The manager replied, 'Yes. He's terrific. But why would you ask?' The programmer said, 'I just wanted to find out how I was doing.'[5]

Another possibility is that it is your methods of working that your boss finds irritating. Perhaps you waste too much of her time asking questions you should find the answers to through other means. Perhaps you do too much social talking on the phone. Perhaps you always leave things dangerously to the last minute. Perhaps you never let her know things she needs to know.

If you suspect this might be so, again the answer is to play psychological detective. Listen carefully to what she says, and observe precisely what events precipitate outbursts of anger and annoyance. Therein should lie the clue.

Are you a threat? It may be that your boss feels threatened by you in some way. Perhaps she feels stale and that she hasn't got any ideas any more, while you are fizzing and popping with them like a soda syphon. Perhaps she's jealous because she's not as good at getting arguments over verbally as you are.

The answer here, as with colleagues, is to minimize the competitive element. And you can do more than that – you can emphasize the *cooperative* aspects of your relationship. 'We should really knock their eyes out with this display, shouldn't we?' 'That remark you made about trade-offs really made my task a lot easier.' 'I'd like to ask your advice about how to handle the meeting tomorrow.'

Research suggests that people who see their goals as 'positively linked' – that is, that the goal accomplishment of the one helps the other attain theirs – are more likely to form better and more productive relationships.[6]

Researchers in this area provide few clues as to how you might achieve this 'positive linkage' between your goals if it isn't already built into your job. But the principle makes sense: it is better to emphasize the fact that your goals and your boss's goals overlap rather than to imply that you're both working towards different – or at worst incompatible – ends. The same principle, by the way, applies to relationships between colleagues[7] as well as to how leaders should treat subordinates.[8]

GENERAL RULES FOR HANDLING BOSSES

Many of the points mentioned above apply to all bosses, of course: doing your work well and letting them know it tactfully if it's not obvious; prefacing disagreements with 'you're the boss but'-type statements; saying appreciative things when you can do so genuinely; being sensitive to things that irritate them; emphasizing that you see your relationship as a cooperative one (use the word 'we' whenever you can!).

Michael Argyle and his colleagues, in the course of their research on the rules that people think are important in various relationships (pp. 31–4), asked their English sample about rules for dealing with superiors at work. The list is quite instructive:

1. Don't hesitate to question when orders are unclear.
2. Use initiative where possible.
3. Put forward and defend your own ideas.
4. Complain first to your superior before going to others.
5. Respect the other's privacy.

6. Be willing and cheerful.

7. Don't be too submissive.

8. Be willing to accept criticism.

9. Keep confidences.

10. Be willing to take orders.

11. Don't say derogatory things about your superior.

12. Look your superior in the eye during conversation.

13. Obey your superior's instructions.

14. Don't visit your superior socially unannounced.

15. Don't criticize your superior publicly.'

These rules cover all the vital elements involved in dealing successfully with bosses: making sure you know what they expect of you, doing what they want as far as you think correct and feasible, making their life as easy as you can (for example, by not throwing a major wobbly every time she or he criticizes something you've done) – and being loyal. Loyalty makes bosses feel secure because it makes them feel they are managing their own job all right. They are only human after all.

DEALING WITH CONFLICTS

You notice that I talk about doing what your boss wants 'as far as you think correct and feasible'. Unfortunately, unless you've been monumentally lucky, there will have been times when you thought your boss was talking through the back of his or her head. 'Oh, I'd just like you to do a report on labour problems in the nickel industry of the Lower Kalabash by three o'clock.' 'I *told* you to check those advertising figures. Now we're £100,000 out on the estimates' (when he'd told you he was going to handle them himself). 'By the way, I think you'd better invite Fred along to our meeting this afternoon. He could be very useful on how to deal with the sewerage problem in the Acacia Avenue apartment block' (when you know perfectly well that Fred is a wide boy who would sell his grandmother into slavery for a used fiver, and if he has anything to do with it the occupants of the entire block will go down with typhoid in a week).

Whether you just silently grit your teeth or confront the issue will depend on lots of factors – how much you care about it, whether you feel hard done by, how high the stakes are, and so on.

In cases of really serious conflict, an American researcher, Steven Musser, has outlined five main strategies that subordinates are likely to use:

1. '*Problem solving: let's lay our cards on the table and work this thing out.*' The most likely choice if (a) you want to stay in your job and (b) you feel that your superior interprets the facts and regards them in the same light as you do. For example, you may both agree on the importance of not being £100,000 out on next year's estimates, and it's only the details of how it happened that pose the difficulty.

2. '*Bargaining: give and take.*' Most likely strategy if (a) you want to stay in the organization, (b) you do *not* share your boss's attitudes and beliefs on the issue in question, and (c) you have enough power to protect you from arbitrary action on your boss's part (such as disciplining you, not promoting or even sacking you).

3. '*Appeasing (ingratiating): "I'm sorry, you're right".*' The probable choice if (a) you want to keep your job, (b) you do not share your boss's attitudes, and (c) you have *no* protection or redress against any arbitrary action he or she might take.

4. '*Competing: "I did it my way".*' Only likely to be chosen if (a) you actually don't care whether you stay in your organization or not, but (b) you share your superior's beliefs on the issue and feel it's worth making a stand, if only to protect your own self-esteem.

5. '*Withdrawing: "You can take this job and . . ."*' Hardly
   needs any explanation, does it?[10]

This model of how subordinates are likely to react has not
yet been tested, nor is it prescriptive; it is about what is likely
to happen, not what would be the best strategy. But I think
it is useful in that it draws attention to factors it might be as
well to think carefully about if things are really hot: how
much do you need this job? Do you and your supervisor
generally see work issues in the same way? Do you have any
protection against the boss taking punitive action against
you?

Fortunately, most conflicts with the boss will not be of the
make-or-break kind. They'll be of the 'It's time you learned
there is such a thing as a filing system, Jenkins' and 'Why the
hell haven't you rung Dr Mugwort yet?' variety.

Apologizing

If the problem is simply that you've made a blunder, apolo-
gize. Don't avoid apologies on the ostrich-like ground that
somehow if you're out of sight you won't get blamed. The
evidence is that apologizing does help to avert the fires of
bossly wrath.

Terence Mitchell and Robert Wood, psychologists and
management experts at the University of Washington, have
certainly found it to work. In experiments they gave nurse
supervisors descriptions of incidents of poor performance by
nurses. These ranged from things like giving a patient too
much of a dangerous drug to failing to put up the side railing
on a patient's bed.

Obviously, the worse the outcome, the more punitive the
supervisors said they would be. But if the nurse reportedly
said she was sorry the supervisors were less severe. They had
higher future expectations of her, more confidence in her
ability and would supervise her in future less closely than if
she had not apologized.

In another experiment students were asked to play the roles of supervisors and subordinates and to discuss a missed production deadline. 'Supervisors' were less punitive if they were given an explanation of 'external' circumstances ('necessary materials had been somewhat late arriving from another department') than if the cause were 'internal' to the employee (who had 'extended his or her lunch hour by 45 minutes to talk with a friend').

Clearly the account offered has to be acceptable and believable. If so, 'By offering accounts,' Mitchell and his colleagues say, 'the subordinate may get the leader to disassociate the evaluation of the poor performance from an evaluation of his or her moral character and potential for future performance'.[11]

Apologizing and pointing out to your boss various factors in the situation that he or she might not be aware of (this is vital, as the chances are they won't be aware of them or will underplay their importance, as we saw in the last chapter) will at least serve as 'damage limitation' tactics.

Assertiveness

Conflicts are not always triggered by your mistakes, however. And sometimes the circumstances are such that it would be best if you could just stand up and say what you think. After all, is it fair that a bunch of innocents should get typhoid just because Fred has got some scam going with the sewerage people? Is it reasonable that you should be expected to produce 10,000 words on the wretched nickel industry in Lower Kalabash in half a day flat? And should you take the blame for doing what the boss told you just because it all went hideously wrong?

Easier said than done of course, and courses on assertiveness training are multiplying like rabbits in spring. But just knowing some of the principles might help.

The first thing is to define what assertiveness actually is.

It's usually taken to mean 'the legitimate and honest expression of one's personal rights, feelings, beliefs, and interests without violating or denying the rights of others'.[12]

It is important to distinguish this from aggression, which is another animal altogether. As the American social psychologists Kay Deaux and Lawrence Wrightsman put it:

> In many interactions, we disagree with the statements or actions of another person. How do we respond? Recently, many advocates of assertiveness training have suggested that there are three possible responses to most situations: a passive response, an aggressive response, or an assertive response. The passive response is to do nothing – to inhibit one's own feelings for fear of offending the other person. An aggressive response, in contrast, directly attacks the other person. With the third possibility, the assertive response, a person can make his or her feelings known without attacking the other person.[13]

An example. Let's imagine how these might work.

BOSS: 'I thought that meeting you organized yesterday was an absolute shambles.'

Passive response: 'Erm, yes, well, I'm dreadfully sorry, I don't know how it happened, it just seemed to . . . I'll – um . . .' (backs out, miserable).

Aggressive response: 'Well, what the hell do you expect, given the ludicrous brief I was given?'

Assertive response: 'I realize it might have seemed like that. But I thought giving everyone the opportunity to air their views freely would be quite valuable. Janet came up to me afterwards, for example, and said she'd be rethinking the inflatable mongoose sales forecast.'

Of the three possible responses, being assertive is regarded as the best because although it doesn't guarantee you'll get what you want, it will give you a much better chance of doing so. You will at least get out of the situation with your self-esteem intact; and you won't have generated – or accelerated – waves of hostility that could seriously damage your relationship with the other person. (Assertiveness techniques, of course, are designed for dealings with your colleagues, subordinates and indeed everyone in your life – not just the boss.)

Assertiveness skills. Assertiveness experts classify the skills involved in different ways, but all are essentially about saying straightforwardly what you really feel, at the same time as recognizing that the other person has rights and feelings too. You might disagree with what they are *saying*, but you should avoid belittling them as *people*. 'I disagree with that point' is better than 'How in God's name could you possibly suggest such a thing? Moron.'

It may also be that there are some points buried in the critical thicket that are correct or justified. By talking about the problem directly you are much more likely to disentangle them.

Allen Appell of San Francisco State University describes four assertiveness skills:

1. *Self-disclose*. This means 'you objectively state what you feel and want'. For instance: 'I feel this program is the best' beats 'I don't know. Some people think this program might be better', which is, Appell says firmly, 'wishy-washy'.

2. *Persist*. 'You must now be prepared to *persist*; that is, to maintain your position in the face of unfair criticism and manipulation.'

3. *Affirm*. Will being objective and not personally judging or attacking the other person work in the face of their aggression? 'You can withstand a verbal onslaught just as a sapling can bend with the wind and prevail against a storm,' Appell says. 'You can do so by agreeing with, or affirming, the other person's right to express an opinion.' After a heavy artillery attack from the boss, resist the

temptation to whip out a Kleenex or pass out. You can say, 'I know it seems like that but . . .' or 'I appreciate why you might think that but . . .' or, if you actually agree with them, 'You're right! Next time I'll . . .'

4. *Reflect*. This means you repeat back to them what you think they're saying. 'So you feel that . . .?' allows them to see more clearly what they have said, including any illogicalities or exaggerations; it enables you to check that you've understood correctly what they meant; and it shows that you're making an effort to do so.

The first letter of each heading forms the acronym SPAR, Appell points out. A bit too aggressive, really, but a useful aid to memory . . .[14]

The 'self-disclose' and 'affirm' elements are crucial ones that keep cropping up whenever assertiveness techniques are outlined. Ken and Kate Back, two management training consultants who specialize in assertiveness courses, refer to them as 'basic assertion' and 'empathetic assertion' respectively.

The first is 'a straightforward statement that stands up for your rights by making clear your needs, wants, beliefs, opinions or feelings'. For example: 'As I see it the system is working well.' 'I need to be away by five o'clock.' 'I feel very pleased with the way the issue has been resolved.'

The second variety adds in 'an element of empathy': 'I appreciate that you don't like the new procedure. However, until it's changed I'd like you to keep your people working to it.' 'I know you're busy at the moment, John, but I'd like to make a quick request of you.'

Ken and Kate Back recommend that you don't make the empathetic approach into a ritual. 'It is easy to over-use phrases like "I appreciate your feelings on this, but . . ." so that the currency of empathy is debased.' You're not, in other words, really taking the other person's views or feelings into account at all. But empathy is, they argue, 'an essential ingredient for resolving conflicts in which people are behaving aggressively'. [15]

How do people react to assertiveness? Even though assertiveness sounds a good idea from your point of view, do other people really want you to behave like that? Wouldn't they rather you were non-assertive and wimpish? And if you're a woman, isn't being assertive a bit – well, you know, not *done*?

A few studies have implied that assertiveness is not likely to make you as popular as being passive.[16] But there is evidence that you *can* say what you want without being cast into some sort of social outer darkness. In an article on assertiveness in work contexts American psychologists Regis McNamara and Ronald Delamater offer some reassurance.[17] They quote, for example, a study published in 1982 in which male and female corporate managers, with an average of twenty years' experience on the job, listened to audiotapes of a man and a woman handling common business situations:[18] 'Results showed that self-effacing behavior by models of both sexes was rated less favorably than either direct assertiveness or empathic assertiveness. Assertive male and female models were rated as comparably likeable, socially skilled, and interpersonally effective.'[19]

More artificial laboratory research produces similar results. An experiment with students, for example, found that they preferred assertive and empathic-assertive rather than passive behaviour in people they knew, and they rated passive responses higher than aggressive and 'passive-aggressive' (passive obstruction or sarcasm) ones.

With familiar people, both types of assertion were rated as being 'more comfortable to receive, as being the most likely responses to gain their compliance, and were seen by their receivers as the most likely to enhance relationships with the speakers'. (The undergraduates were not quite so keen on empathic assertiveness from complete strangers, probably because it was seen as being a bit presumptuous. They also rated passivity as highly as direct assertiveness in strangers, while any form of aggression got a major thumbs down.)[20]

INFLUENCE TACTICS

What about more subtle tactics for getting your own way with the boss? Sadly, psychologists have not come up with lists of the most effective strategies. There are a few studies of the techniques people use on their bosses, but they do not give any evidence as to which are the most successful ones.[21]

For example, psychologist David Kipnis of Temple University, Philadelphia, and his colleagues asked managers on part-time graduate business courses to describe how they tried to influence their bosses, co-workers and subordinates. 'Men and women,' the researchers say, 'chose similar tactics when attempting to get their way.'

The top reason for trying to influence the boss was to initiate change. For example, to get him or her 'to accept a new way of doing the work more efficiently or a new program or project'. And, unsurprisingly, compared to colleagues and subordinates, bosses were the most likely targets of attempts to obtain personal benefits – 'such as raises, better hours of work, time off, better job assignments, and so on'.

To gain such benefits, the most popular tactics were 'exchange' and 'ingratiation'. 'Exchange' was measured by tactics such as:

1. Offering an exchange (e.g., if you do this for me, I will do something for you).
2. Offering to make a personal sacrifice if the other would do what you want (e.g., working late, working harder, etc.).
3. Doing personal favours for the other.

'Ingratiation' covered items such as:

1. Making the other feel important ('only you have the brains, talent to do this').
2. Acting in a friendly manner prior to asking for what you want.
3. Making the other feel good about you before making your request.

When managers tried to get their boss to initiate change, in addition to 'exchange' and 'ingratiation' they used two other tactics: 'rationality' and 'coalition'. The 'rationality' tactics were as follows:

1. Writing a detailed plan justifying your ideas.
2. Presenting the other with information in support of your point of view.
3. Explaining the reasons for your request.
4. Using logic to convince the other.
5. Writing a memo describing what you want.
6. Offering to compromise over the issue (giving in a little).
7. Demonstrating your competence before making your request.[22]

'Coalition' referred to getting the support of co-workers and/ or subordinates to back up the request.

Although these are not prescriptive lists, they do concentrate the mind on possible strategies. The ones chosen will depend on many factors, such as your relationship with the boss, the precise circumstances, and so on. So will their effectiveness: if you say 'Boss, angel, my productivity's up 150 per cent and don't you think I deserve a raise?' and the boss has only recently had a rocket on the subject of his department's costs, the answer will be no even if you offer to feed his budgie every day into the bargain.

But one American study has tried to tease out which strategies seem to be involved in successful attempts, and which in unsuccessful ones. Most, as you might expect, sometimes worked and sometimes didn't. 'Using group or peer support', for example, was not used significantly more often in successful than in unsuccessful attempts to influence the boss; nor was 'logically presenting ideas', the most commonly reported technique.

What did seem to distinguish successful from unsuccessful attempts, according to the researchers' sample of supervisors, was having a good interpersonal relationship in the first place. This was especially true in small organizations. Perhaps in small companies supervisors have more room to manoeuvre than in rigidly run large companies, and can take their personal feelings about their subordinates more into account.

Of all the influence tactics, the only one that the supervisors overwhelmingly put in the 'much more often successful than not' camp was 'trading job-related benefits' – in other words, the 'exchange' strategy.[23]

These findings – which applied to both men and women – reinforce what we already know about how important it is to develop a good, trusting relationship with your boss. And when you want him or her to do something for you, it is a good idea to *offer something in return*. This makes a lot of psychological sense, in view of the widely held rule of social life which makes us feel we should reciprocate when we are offered or given something.

So when you next present a request to your boss, try something like this: 'I feel eminently suited to take over the development of the new high-fibre chocolate bar (because of my long acquaintance with the cocoa bean, my brilliance, my medical contacts, etc., etc.). If you handed it over to me, it would save you having to talk to that *desperately* boring market research man who always brings you out in hives.'

HANDLING THE BOSS IF YOU ARE A WOMAN

Being a woman can lead to difficulties with your boss that are greater than your male colleagues have to face. If the boss is male, there's the risk of sexual harassment; if the boss is sexist, that has to be dealt with.

As a result, there may be extra pressure on you to perform well. In their study of British women managers, Cary Cooper and Marilyn Davidson quote a junior marketing executive on her male bosses:

> They do tend to treat me differently than my male colleagues as my bosses tend to rely on me more as I think they see me as being more efficient. Pressure is tremendous to be better than a male. If a man forgot to do something people tend to think, 'Oh well, he can do it tomorrow' but if it were me, they may think, 'Oh, it's that woman again'. I make sure I'm better, I don't slip up, I don't forget anything.[24]

The strain may be even worse if you are a 'token' woman in a male environment. You may find yourself forced into a role that is hardly that of a respected colleague, such as 'pet', 'mother', 'seductress' or 'iron maiden' (i.e., dangerous feminist).[25]

Breaking the stereotypes. The kind of stereotypes that can cause problems for women in male-dominated jobs and occupations[26] will, I believe, slowly collapse under sustained onslaught.[27] As more and more women move into such professions and struggle their way upwards, the less the fact that a colleague *is* a woman will matter. Sex will become a less obvious criterion for judging women than when there are only one or two to be sighted around the office.

In the meantime, all one can really do is not to let your boss/colleagues/subordinates get away with remarks implying that your sex is somehow relevant to your work:

BOSS: 'I'll have your husband on to me if I ask you to work late on this rush job.'

YOU: 'My husband is fine about things like that – isn't your wife?'

BOSS: 'I just don't think women are as good as men at giving presentations. I mean, you all get so nervous.'

YOU: 'That's not true at all. In fact, I *enjoy* giving presentations!'

And, when you're in mid-flight on a fluent description of your latest project, you get 'Wow, you're looking really attractive today' (a classic put-down of the 'Hey, you're forgetting you're only a woman' type), you could try 'Nice of you to say so – I like your suit too – but as I was saying . . .' It's vital to *act*, and to make it clear that you expect to be treated as a valued colleague worthy of respect.

Taking action. In *Strategies for Women at Work*, an American career consultant, Janice LaRouche, with editor Regina Ryan, list twenty-seven kinds of problem you can have with the boss (most of which men may suffer from too, in fact). They range from 'I do all the work and my boss takes all the credit' and 'My boss is threatened by me' to 'My boss makes sexual overtures' and My boss is a chauvinist slob'.[28]

LaRouche and Ryan believe that it's vital to realize there are *things you can do* when times are bad. It would be very rare for a woman to be so hopelessly entrapped in a situation that there is no course of action she could take to alleviate matters. There is, indeed, evidence that believing your life is under your own control is more psychologically beneficial than feeling you are at the mercy of fate and outside circumstances.[29]

An example. LaRouche and Ryan cite some quite stylish examples of ways action can be taken. In the 'I do all the work and my boss takes all the credit' problem area:

> One of my clients, a stage manager, was distressed to discover that the producer of a show she'd worked on had,

in a fit of pique, left her title off the show's program. That credit was critical for her future job hunts. I suggested that she go to a printer and have a new program made up for her own use – one that would accurately reflect her involvement in the production. The new program would be exactly like the old one, except that it would bear one additional line: 'Mary Jones . . . stage manager'. My client's reaction to my suggestion was, at first, horror. She felt she'd be doing something virtually illegal. But her initial reaction was soon replaced with delight when I persuaded her that her program would be the accurate one, and that no one, including the producer, was likely to call her to task for telling the truth – a truth that could easily be verified by all who had worked on the show.[30]

Rather an extreme example, naturally, but the point is there: even when things look very black, you *can* do something. And in your everyday dealings with your boss, remember that you are not helpless. You and your boss are bound together in a web of obligations and responsibilities; and the boss needs skills, competence, productivity and loyalty from you just as you need rewards, encouragement and feedback from him or her.

Decisions – how to make them

I really don't know what to do. I've got to decide how to deal with all this work my boss has been piling on to me. Should I object? Should I use it as an argument for a new assistant? But will that be taken as a sign of weakness? Is there anything I can drop from my current workload? Frankly it's keeping me awake at nights. Everything just keeps going round and round . . .

I'm in a dreadful dilemma. I need a raise. I deserve a raise. But the last secretary who asked for one got the sack. What should I do? I mean, I just have to ladder my tights to think Oh God, there's the price of a frozen pizza down the drain . . .

This decision is absolutely crucial. If we make the wrong move with the Kittyfood people, there's our biggest account gone. And yet we can't go along with their latest ludicrous idea on hang-gliding tomcats, we'd be had up before the RSPCA. But departmental meetings don't have too good a record on sensible decisions. Remember that time everyone went along with Jim's idea to erect a giant whisky bottle by that beautiful Scottish loch as a publicity stunt? You know, the place that turned out to be completely unreachable by any known form of transport? Nightmare.

Making decisions can give us a lot of anxiety. The microdecisions of office life, of course, we don't need to get overfretful about. Whether to go to the sandwich shop or wallow in lasagne at the local Italian is not going to strain the brain excessively. But not-so-trivial decisions demand serious thinking; and, unfortunately, psychologists have found that we're not as wonderful at decision-making as we think we are.

INDIVIDUAL DECISION-MAKING

The ideal, rational decision-maker, psychologists say,[1] would approach any decision like this:

1. Research all the relevant information intensively.
2. Consider *all* possible alternative courses of action.
3. Think of *all* the possible consequences of each alternative.
4. Estimate the chances of each alternative leading to each possible outcome.
5. Assign a value to each outcome: i.e., work out how valuable and desirable it is.
6. Combine the probability estimates and outcome values for each alternative.
7. Choose the course of action that is most likely to bring you what you most want.

Well, surprise surprise, the evidence is that we rarely manage to do this.

Think of all the options. For a start, we find it enormously difficult – if not impossible – to think of all the possible courses of action we might take, never mind all their consequences.

Psychologist Charles Gettys of the University of Oklahoma and his colleagues, for example, gave students the task of thinking of all possible actions that might effectively solve the problem of insufficient parking space at the university. Between them the students generated a large number of potential solutions. These ranged from 'put "small car" spaces in student parking lots' and 'reschedule activities and/or classes to spread demand more evenly over time' to 'sell low-priced bicycles' and off-the-wall suggestions like 'saying that the Surgeon General has found cars cancerous'.

'The acts generated by our subjects,' the researchers say, 'usually included at least one reasonable action, and sometimes included several good actions. Therefore, we do not feel that our subjects are doomed to a life of taking ineffectual actions. This level of performance is satisfactory for solving trivial problems in a benign environment.'

But, they say darkly, where problems are ill-defined and the costs of making poor decisions are high, the generating of possible solutions is 'substantially incomplete'. What's more, the evidence is that having thought of a possible course of action, you might still have difficulty imagining the potential consequences. Gettys and his associates suggest that importing a specially trained 'decision analyst' might help.[2] However, this is not on the cards in the normal hurly-burly of office life.

What this research clearly reveals is that we need to work hard at generating possible courses of action, and when we think we've thought of everything, we need to have yet one more think. (The students in these experiments were more pleased with their performance than was in fact warranted.) And when we've thought of as many solutions as we can, we need to try to work out all the possible costs as well as the benefits of each one.

Draw up a balance-sheet. Psychologists Irving Janis and Leon Mann have suggested exhaustively listing all the advantages and disadvantages of each alternative before trying to make the decision.[3] This 'balance-sheet' idea will not only help clarify your thinking but may perhaps encourage you to take into account considerations that you might otherwise have ignored. 'Well, a good thing about telling the boss that I saw one of his favourite clients lunching at the Savoy with his deadly rival from Megafunk and Co. is that he'll see me as a loyal sidekick with my ear to the ground and a line on what's happening. But then he might ask me what the hell *I* was doing at the Savoy at lunchtime on my salary . . .'

Janis and Mann's technique does not incorporate any way of weighting and combining all the various points, as decision theorists recommend. There are complex ways of doing this,[4] but unless the decision is of really major proportions and you have a decision analyst to advise you, you'll have to forget them and rely on drawing up 'pros' and 'cons' columns on the backs of used envelopes.

In practice, for most decisions, you are quite likely to find yourself weighing up the pros and cons of a rather meagre set of alternatives. Herbert Simon, a renowned expert on decision-making, has pointed out that in real life (as opposed to the rational 'ideal' world) decision-makers typically fix on the first solution they come to that is just good enough, although not the best one possible.[5]

This may often be fine. Janis and Mann have suggested that for decisions that are not terribly fundamental, that have to be made quickly and that are easy to reverse, it's sensible to settle on an acceptable – if not the best – option.[6] To do so rapidly you would probably consider a restricted number of alternatives and consequences. Perhaps only one. 'Ring our lawyer immediately and just do whatever she tells you. That'll give us a breathing-space . . .'

But decisions aren't always so unimportant. And unfortunately, the evidence is that people can cut off the search for alternatives much too early. The Israeli psychologist Arie Kruglanski calls this 'freezing' on to a decision. 'It truncates the information-search phase of the decision-making process,' he says, 'during which a person actively considers all available options before making a final judgment.'

Why does this happen? Kruglanski thinks freezing is more likely when a person doesn't 'have access to evidence that the judgment could be incorrect'; when wishful thinking makes a desirable option seem even more desirable; or when any decision seems better than uncertainty.

An example. Kruglanski's analysis of the tragedy of the space shuttle *Challenger*, which exploded in 1986 killing seven people, illustrates how freezing can work. There was a problem with information:

> In the case of Challenger, the compartmentalized deliberation process at NASA kept information – such as the presence of cold spots on a booster rocket – from being transmitted to the responsible officials, making it easier for them to freeze their commitment to launch.

Wishful thinking also played its part:

> People often engage in wishful thinking, believing what they find convenient or desirable . . . Lift-off was clearly more desirable than delay. A 'go' decision meant that the flight schedule could be kept, that the public would not be disappointed and that the shuttle program would score another major achievement. Also, any mention of possible system failure would have suggested the need to spend more money, a conclusion NASA found distasteful in light of its commitment to cost-effectiveness and economy.

People often prefer clear-cut answers to problems, too:

> Since indecision and ambiguity are stressful, any decision seems better than delay. This need for structure increases as a deadline draws near – precisely the condition that faced NASA officials with the Challenger.

There is, however, a factor that works against freezing, Kruglanski argues – a 'fear of invalidity'. 'When the perceived costs of a bad decision or judgment seem high, a decision-maker is likely to search for alternatives and is particularly sensitive to information about the flaws and pitfalls of a decision.' Sadly, this process was not operating at the time of the *Challenger* launch decision. 'This fear seemed to be lost in a general atmosphere of enthusiasm; no one wanted to be reminded that any kind of accident was possible.'[7]

The *Challenger* mission is a particularly dramatic example, but the psychological processes, if we're honest, are all too familiar. The implications for how we make decisions are clear:

1. Search as hard as you can in the time available for information relevant to the problem.

2. Be especially alert to the information with negative implications for the option you most lean towards. Don't ignore its possible bad consequences just because you don't want to have to think about it. As psychologists Robert Abelson and Ariel Levi say, 'A decision maker already committed to a particular alternative is ordinarily not disposed to scan that course of action for hidden drawbacks.'[8] And examine why it is your favourite option: is there a strong element of wishful thinking in there?

3. Try not to feel that, within the constraints of the time available, any delay in making the decision and having everything settled is unbearable. It would be better to use the time to search for more information and generate more options than adopt the 'any decision is better than delay' line.

The possibility of bias

If we are to search out relevant information thoroughly, we have to try to conquer our natural biases. We have a tendency to notice – and remember – things that support our beliefs more than those that don't. If we're under high stress and already have a preferred alternative, we may actually *avoid* information that undermines it.[9]

Take the case of your over-demanding boss at the beginning of this chapter. At heart what you really want to do is dump him in the ordure, and so you will leap excitedly at evidence that his own superior quite likes you and may be willing to play the white knight on your behalf. But you may turn a blind eye to information reaching your ears that your boss's superior is going to be transferred soon and your boss is next in line for the job . . .

We are pretty bad at estimating possibilities too. The Israeli psychologists Amos Tversky and Daniel Kahneman have discovered that, without being aware of it, people follow certain 'heuristic principles' that serve to make the difficult task of assessing probabilities a lot easier. (A heuristic is a mental short-cut or rule of thumb.) 'In general,' they write, 'these heuristics are quite useful, but sometimes they lead to severe and systematic errors.'

'Availability'. Tversky and Kahneman call one of these principles the 'availability heuristic'. This means that the easier a possibility is to envisage – the more 'available' it is to your memory – the more likely you think it is to happen.[10] So if you have heard that your boss's last secretary asked for a raise and got the sack instead, this powerful image will lead you to over-estimate the chances of a similar occurrence happening to you. But how many of the boss's staff have asked for a raise and *not* got the sack? And do you know what really happened during that fatal encounter?

The 'availability heuristic' will serve us well a lot of the time, because certain possibilities spring to mind precisely because they *are* frequent. But this is not always so, and it can lead us astray.

Throwing good after bad. Another tendency which psychologists have unearthed is rather endearingly called the 'knee deep in the Big Muddy' phenomenon. This refers to a tendency whereby, after considerable investment – material and/or psychological – in an earlier decision that is turning out badly, we decide to continue or even upgrade the investment. That way we justify the initial decision.

American psychologist Joel Brockner and his colleagues cite some examples of such 'entrapping dilemmas':

> Having already made an initial financial allocation to some high-risk borrowers, the bank loan officer must decide whether to approve an additional loan, when the borrowers later claim that the initial loan will not be sufficient; having already spent hundreds of dollars to repair a car's transmission, buy new tires, and replace the shocks, the car owner must decide whether to spend additional money – now that the brakes require immediate replacement; having already lost thousands of lives, the United States government must decide whether to continue its involvement in a military conflict (e.g., Vietnam).[11]

It's important to be aware of the 'Big Muddy' phenomenon so that you can think through whether or not you should cut your losses. It may well be that what is really holding you back is a desire to save face over the initial decision. The best solution may be not to throw good (money, time, resources) after bad and get into an even worse mess, but to justify that initial decision some other way.

So, for example, you could announce firmly to your colleagues: 'I decided at that time to lend Doggygems Ltd the sum they asked for because profits were rising steadily and their market research indicated a strong interest in costume jewellery for canines. Now they want more money, but in my opinion the market forces have changed and the information I based my judgement on then is now out of date. The new austerity fashions mean that the idea just isn't going to take off, I'm afraid.'

Know your biases. There are no instant panaceas for trouble-some decision-making, but, as Arie Kruglanski says, 'Increasing people's awareness of the process that leads to biased judgments increases their ability to resist those biases.'[12] If you aren't aware of the pitfalls, how can you stop yourself falling into them?

Individual creativity

To make effective decisions, then, it helps to generate as many alternative courses of action as possible. Sometimes, as part of your job, you have to come up with new ideas. In other words, you have to think creatively. Are there any ways you can help yourself to do this better?

The first point to realize is that you shouldn't just lean back with a resigned sigh and say, 'Well, some people are creative and others aren't. And I'm just not.' It's not that easy. Creativity is not simply a matter of personality, as psychologists now recognize.

The current view is that creativity stems from a mixture of factors. For example: general cognitive (thinking) skills; special talents; personality characteristics related to independence and a predisposition to take risks; social factors such as the presence or absence of constraints or incentives, which can affect how motivated you feel; and specific cognitive factors, such as knowing a great deal about the particular problem area and applying psychological tactics that might help you to break out of a limited and conventional way of looking at things.[13]

Some of these factors are under your own control. The more relevant information you have about the subject, for instance, the better your chances of coming up with creative solutions. As psychologist Teresa Amabile wryly puts it, 'It is impossible to be creative in nuclear physics unless one knows something (and probably a great deal) about nuclear physics.'[14]

But what 'thought tactics' might you bring to bear?

Individual brainstorming. The most famous and well researched of all problem-solving techniques, brainstorming, is both simple and effective. It was developed in the 1940s and '50s by a businessman, Alex Osborn. Psychologist Ken Gilhooly of the University of Aberdeen, in his book *Thinking*, describes the method like this:

> Osborn adopts the standard view that problem-solving and creative thinking involve (1) problem formulation, (2) idea-finding and (3) evaluation of ideas to find a likely solution. Brainstorming aims at facilitating the middle, idea-finding stage and it can be summarized as involving 2 main principles and 4 rules.

Principles
1. Deferment of judgment.
2. Quantity breeds quality.

Rules
1. Criticism is ruled out.
2. Free wheeling is welcomed.
3. Quantity wanted.
4. Combination and improvement sought.[15]

The technique was originally designed for use in groups, but it can be used by individuals too. It is based on the idea that our normal method of producing ideas – which involves evaluating each one as it springs to mind – is inhibiting. You might prematurely discard notions that might not work in themselves but that might lead on to others that would. Or you might settle on one idea when a better one is just around the psychological corner.

The theory is that you generate as many ideas as possible without wondering whether they're any good or not, and only when you dry up do you go back through them. The more ideas you produce, the better the chances that at least one of them will be a scorcher.

If you find yourself thinking things like: 'The best way to make dog jewellery fashionable is to try to get the Queen's corgis into ruby-studded anklets,' don't mentally slap yourself for being so silly and wipe it out of your mind. Write it down and keep going. When you go back over all the ideas later, it might strike you that maybe the Queen's corgis are a bit over-ambitious, but what about the winner of this year's Cruft's . . .?

Waiting until you're in the mood. Don't. We tend to think that to do our creative thinking we have to wait until 'the mood comes upon us'. Sadly, what evidence there is implies that the best way to be creative is to force yourself to work at it. One American psychologist, Robert Boice, looked directly at this question with twenty-seven 'blocked' writers who had sought treatment from him to increase their output. Boice was interested in finding the best way of getting them to improve both the quantity of their writing and their production of creative ideas.

He divided the writers – all 'academicians from local campuses' – into three groups. Group 1 were instructed to schedule times for writing five times a week, but to write only if they 'felt like it'. This 'baseline phase' lasted for a minimum of ten scheduled writing days, and ended when they had written nothing on at least three consecutive writing days.

At the end of that phase, the academics agreed to start producing three pages a day. To give them an incentive they were asked to make out five $15 cheques to an organization they despised. On any day when they didn't meet their target, a cheque was mailed by a third person. This phase lasted for at least six weeks.

Group 2 also completed a 'baseline phase' for a fixed period of fifteen writing days. They were then 'informed that although they should continue writing when they felt like it, it was time to begin writing more and that they might accomplish this by stopping to consider doing some writing at each scheduled writing time'. They were to continue 'this regular expectation of doing more writing' for at least twenty scheduled days.

Group 3 were asked to defer any but 'absolutely necessary' writing tasks for ten weeks. This was simply to check how much writing academics would really have to do during this period, to act as a comparison.

The results showed that Group 1, who had been 'forced' to write, 'not only produced more written copy but also generated more creative ideas for writing than did subjects who wrote spontaneously'. Group 2, who were encouraged to write more, but were not pressured to do so, produced only a modest increase (compared with baseline levels) in their number of written pages, and 'reported moderate levels of creative ideas'. Group 3 produced minimal amounts of professional writing and creative ideas.[16]

The findings of this study confirm what many good novelists say about their working methods – that in general they work every day for a fixed number of hours rather than simply waiting for the muse to descend.

Being creative therefore demands effort. So, although Boice's is just one study, and only looked at writing, the idea that you need to schedule a certain time every day when you force yourself to do your creative work – if deadlines permit – makes sense.

If what you are trying to do is to find the best solution to an extremely tricky problem, however, there may have to be a slight qualification. If you find yourself totally stuck, and again if time permits, stopping for a while and then starting again may be a good plan. The reason is to allow for 'incubation'.

Incubation. It has been suggested that there are four basic stages to creative problem-solving:

1. *Preparation*, when you familiarize yourself with all aspects of the problem and do a lot of work on it. 'Much personal testimony,' says Ken Gilhooly, 'indicates that inspiration will not be forthcoming without this preliminary labour; or as Edison, the prolific inventor, is reported to have said, "No inspiration without perspiration".'

2. *Incubation*, when the task is put aside and you do no conscious work on it.

3. *Illumination or inspiration* – the 'Eureka' stage – when a terrific idea springs to mind. Not necessarily the complete solution, but on the right lines.

4. *Verification*, when you do conscious work on the idea to develop and test it.

These four phases are not rigid, and you may cycle between them or be in different phases for different aspects of the problem.[17]

The really interesting question is, what is going on during the incubation period? As Ken Gilhooly points out, 'The notion of incubation plays a prominent role in the recollections of artists and scientists,'[18] yet there have been few experimental studies of the phenomenon. There are, however, signs that it may be most useful for very difficult problems. As to why it can work, there are two main competing ideas:

1. The mind is working on the problem unconsciously.

2. The rest period allows unproductive ways of looking at the problem to fade, so when you look at it again you might see it from a fresh angle.

Psychologists don't yet know the answer, but there are some leanings towards the second explanation.[19] Nevertheless, whatever the reason, it may be that putting a seemingly intractable problem aside for a time might help you out of a psychological rut. It needn't necessarily be that long, either. Haven't you had that experience of going to bed at night with your thoughts about a problem in a tangled knot, and when you wake in the morning you find you suddenly have the solution?

So when in a state, incubate.

GROUP DECISION-MAKING

Making decisions and producing ideas on your own is, of course, only part of the jolly ferment of office life. Another inescapable part involves Meetings. 'Oh God, not another meeting. Chris always drones on and on, half of us never get a chance to say anything and the boss always settles on the most idiotic decisions. It's all such a waste of *time*.'

But it's no good, you can't get away from them. Meetings with colleagues, bosses, subordinates, clients, visitors ... They can be notoriously unproductive, or all too disastrously productive. (You probably know the old adage that a camel is a horse designed by committee ...)

What can be done to improve matters?

Individuals v. groups

The first question is, are there some decision-making tasks that are really done better by individuals than by groups?

There is evidence that if a lot of creative ideas are needed, brainstorming groups will produce the goods better than groups without such instructions. But asking the members of a group to brainstorm *on their own* and then collecting together the results has been found to produce even more ideas – and more good ideas.[20] Even when brainstorming, people gathered together in groups may still feel some inhibitions about letting their imaginations roam.

For solving problems and making decisions, however, groups may frequently be better than individuals because they have more information and a wider range of angles on the problem than one person alone. But this is by no means guaranteed, and groups frequently fail to do as well as they could.[21]

What are the reasons for this? And how can you make
your meetings more effective? (Although the following discussion is mainly aimed at those who run meetings, if you
usually participate rather than chair them you may still find
it very helpful to understand more about how decision-
making groups work. You may sometimes be able to turn
that knowledge to your own and the group's advantage –
we'll focus more on how to influence groups as a participant
in the next chapter.)

Group composition and size

To make full use of the fact that you're making a decision
with the help of a meeting, or else allowing the group itself to
decide, you need to compose the group accordingly. As far as
possible, the members of the group should between them
have all the skills and knowledge relevant to the problem.

Suppose the problem is to ship 800 tons of exotic spices
from India to Southampton in the shortest possible time,
avoiding pirate waters and difficult port authorities. Simon,
for example, might know about the busiest shipping routes;
Babs about pirate raiding areas; Joan about port authorities;
David could be the one in constant contact with the Meteor-
ological Office; Mr Simpson could be the representative of
the client, who would be able, with persuasion, to let you
know what the *real* final deadline was.

You also have to be quite careful about numbers. If you
have fewer than five or six people, you may lose out on skills,
knowledge and ideas; and there is an increased danger of a
'majority wins' process developing which will lessen the
chances of the group exploring the full range of possibilities.[22]

But the evidence is that if you go much over five or six
people you won't significantly improve the quality of the
decision.[23] More than that number, and people may feel more
intimidated, to the extent of not expressing all their ideas or,
at the extreme, not uttering a word even though they might

have a lot of useful things to say. More time may have to be spent just coordinating the group discussion.[24]

There may, however, be people in the office who you think would feel miffed to be excluded. So it is best to ask them: 'Neil, I'm holding a meeting tomorrow morning on the spices shipment. Do you want to be in on that one?' If he says yes, then it's worth including him for the sake of smooth office relationships. But he may not be interested and be secretly relieved not to have to go to yet another meeting. So he can say no thanks, and go away with his self-esteem undamaged. You did ask him, after all.

Group processes

Avoid hostility; encourage disagreement. Avoid bringing people together who hate each other. While disagreements in a group can be very productive, hostility is another matter, and may just serve to make everyone less keen on the whole exercise.

What psychologist Dean Tjosvold and his colleagues call 'constructive controversy', in contrast, is to be encouraged. The constructive discussion of opposing opinions, they say, 'appears to contribute substantially to successful decision-making'. The reason is that controversy, when 'productively discussed' (crudely speaking this means listening to rather than trying to outdo each other), 'leads to an exploration of the opposing positions, openminded consideration and understanding of these positions, and a willingness to integrate these ideas into a high quality, accepted [by the group] solution'.[25]

It helps, Tjosvold and his associates find, if the decision-makers feel that they need to cooperate to reach a decision. If you are the person running the meeting, you can try to encourage a 'we are in it together' attitude. It is also important that people should not feel that their personal competence is under attack.

For example, it is vital that disagreement with another's ideas should not be phrased as a rejection of that person. Say 'I think it wouldn't be a good idea actually to bug the offices of Ratpest Inc., Val, but if you can think of something that might have the same effect . . .'; *not* 'What an idiotic suggestion, Val, for heaven's sake.'

Sometimes you might have to make this distinction explicit. To supersensitive Doug, for instance: 'I don't believe that particular strategy would work, Doug. But you're good at coming up with solutions to this kind of problem – anything else occur to you?'

Sometimes, too, it happens that everyone comes to a meeting fighting mad over the issue in question. A friend of mine who was present at such a meeting told me: 'The chairman did all he could do, I suppose. He just avoided discussing the root of the conflict, and said "We'll take that as read, and go on from there".' Although the meeting managed to reach a compromise in the end, it was one that no one was really happy with.

If you find yourself in such a predicament, there is something you can do other than by-passing the whole problem. That is, just to be straight. Say something like: 'Look, I know several of you feel angry about this. But we're not going to be able to sort it out if you all start yelling at each other. I'd like each of you, in turn, quietly to tell the rest of us *exactly* how you see the situation, and no one is to interrupt please. And you should not use your turn to tear into what earlier speakers have said. We want to know *your* perspective on the problem. When everyone's had their say, we will go through the points that have been raised. And while it's fair to disagree with *points* the others have made, personal attacks are not on. OK, Penny, you start.'

Intimidation. Try to watch out for signs that some members of your staff are intimidating others. This may be particularly likely to happen if there are only one or two women in an otherwise male group. British researcher Heather Hemming writes severely: 'Knowledge of subordinates' skills is a better guide to speaker contribution than male sex and high expressive power. Intervention may be required when informal male groups reinforce each other's high power expressive behavior combined with social-sexual behavior towards lone women who cannot retaliate.'[26]

In other words, don't let men hog the floor and interrupt and talk over the women. If you are a woman and you are running the meeting, the men may not try it with you, but that may not stop them from trying it with the lower-status women. Say things like: 'Sue, what do you think?' and 'Bob, I'd like to hear the rest of Sue's point.' It's also important not to let any of the men get away with sexual remarks to beleaguered Sue in their attempts to put her down. (Hopefully Sue won't be in need of any intervention by you . . .)

Conformity. Some people may well remain silent when a dominant group position seems to be emerging, and not speak up when you say 'Right, are we all agreed then?' In groups, there are strong pressures towards conformity, and our desire to be accepted by the group, or not to appear foolish, may override our wish to disagree.

Just how strong these pressures can be was demonstrated in the classic experiments carried out by an American psychologist, Solomon Asch. He would give a group of people, all but one of whom would be his accomplices, a series of simple problems. In each they were shown a line and they had to say which of three other lines of different lengths matched it. The accomplices would give their answers in turn before the subject did, and sometimes unanimously gave what was *clearly* the wrong answer. The critical question was, would the subject go along with them?

The results showed that most subjects resisted conforming

to the group consensus most of the time; but three quarters of them conformed at least once. As Robert Baron and Donn Byrne put it, 'These results, and those obtained in many later studies . . ., point to an unsettling conclusion: many persons find it less upsetting to publicly contradict the evidence of their own senses than to disagree openly with the unanimous judgments of other persons – even those of total strangers.'[27]

Think how much stronger the pressures are when the group is one whose good opinion matters a lot to you – like the group you work with. And in most cases, problems don't have any obviously right or wrong answer anyway; they just have better or worse ones.

It is important, therefore, not to let group pressure prevent possibly important facts, ideas, objections and suggestions being raised. Make sure everyone who has something to say on the topic gets to speak. A person may become diffident when a couple of superconfident loud talkers get enough murmurs of agreement to make it seem that the whole thing is sewn up. So you could say something like: 'Well, I think we ought to hear a few more ideas on this before coming to a conclusion. Clive, what's your view on this? Are there any possible problems you can foresee?'

Don't dominate the group yourself. Another facet of this 'getting everyone to participate' idea is the danger that you yourself will inhibit them. As the person in charge, you are almost certainly going to be of higher status than them. They may feel anxious about the risks they could incur by disagreeing with you.

The American social psychologist, Leonard Berkowitz, gives a rather dramatic example of this process at work:

Throughout his administration (1963 to 1968) President Lyndon B. Johnson took pains to show everyone that he was in charge. The big decisions were his decisions. As in most government matters, he had very decided opinions regarding the conduct of the Vietnam war, and was especially determined to have his way in the face of the mounting domestic criticism of the war in 1966 and 1967.

But he still carried on 'consulting' the National Security Council (NSC) on tactics and strategies.

Many of the NSC meetings were actually only a status-driven ritual. The president would announce his decision and then poll everyone in the room – council members, their assistants, and members of the White House and NSC staffs. Restrained by the president's status, very few people participating in these meetings ever questioned Johnson's decisions or long-term war policies. Whatever their private misgivings, openly they only agreed with him.

The leader's status in this case clearly kept the group from living up to its potential. The NSC was composed of very able people, and some of them had a good deal of experience in southeast Asia. But this talent and knowledge couldn't be brought to bear on the problem facing the group because the members were reluctant to challenge the high-status leader's opinions.[28]

An extreme example, obviously, but the process is probably familiar. To overcome it you'll need to make a strong effort not to state your opinions on the issue *until everyone else has stated theirs*. Otherwise you may just be deafened by the chorus of 'Mm hmms' and you might just as well not have bothered to hold the meeting in the first place. And your staff will go away disgruntled, to boot.

Don't think 'Oh, it's just gentle old me, they know they can say what they like.' You can't be sure of this. Whatever you are like as a person, at work you occupy a 'role', and if you're in the 'boss' or 'powerful' role subordinates may feel an edge of wariness in your presence.

'Group polarization'. Psychologists have discovered that if most of a group of people already lean in a particular direction on an issue before they discuss it – say, that stricter limitations ought to be placed on the sales department's entertaining expenses – then the decision the group makes will often be more extreme than the average of the individuals' personal decisions before they met to talk about it.[29]

Why does this 'group polarization' happen?

A major factor seems to be that when most people in a group incline towards a particular view from the start, the majority of arguments that come out during the group discussion will be in favour of that view. As a result, group members will hear *new* arguments in favour of the position most of them initially preferred, and some of these arguments may also appear to be particularly cogent. 'There may be a gradual shift toward extremity as more and more dissenters change their minds and join the "bandwagon",' Robert Baron says. 'In addition, ideas coming out of the group deliberations can convince people that their initially held views were correct all along, leading them to more strongly endorse the favored course of action.'[30]

Another process thought to be at work is called 'social comparison'. Since we like to see and present ourselves favourably relative to others, we assume that we hold more extreme views in the 'desirable' direction than they do. If our group is generally in favour of curtailing expenses, we reckon we're personally jolly tough-minded on this issue. But when we hear what others have to say we may realize that we are not as 'one up' as we thought, and so we may become even more extreme.[31]

In some circumstances it may be that a more extreme version of members' initial positions *is* the best outcome. But frequently, of course, it may not be. We have seen how essential it is to explore all options thoroughly. If you see your meeting zeroing in on a major decision without too much disagreement, try to resist the temptation to heave a gigantic sigh of relief. It may be that there are other factors that ought to be brought out but which are not being mentioned because of these 'polarizing' group processes.[32] It might be a good plan to poke around for arguments *against* the favoured position, and for some alternatives.

Take those staggering sales department expenses. 'What would be the arguments for keeping the sales department's expenses limit as it is, do you think, Jill? Or are there arguments for actually increasing it? Or being more precise about how much should be spent in different areas? Or being more specific about which restaurants should be chosen? Are there any other possibilities we should be considering?'

'Groupthink'. At the extreme, groups are capable of making quite mind-bogglingly awful decisions. This may sometimes come about because of a process called 'groupthink', which actively prevents a group from thoroughly and objectively considering a wide range of possible alternatives.

Irving Janis of Yale University identified this phenomenon when he analysed political documents on high-level policy decisions that were complete fiascos.[33] He isolated a number of factors that proved extremely detrimental to the making of good decisions:

1. Anybody who expressed severe doubts about the choice preferred by the majority was defined as 'disloyal'.

2. The group members employed 'self-censorship' – in other words, they kept quiet about any doubts or misgivings they had.

3. They had an 'illusion of unanimity' – partly due to self-censorship, partly to a false assumption that silence meant consent.

4. The group suffered from an 'illusion of invulnerability' that made them excessively optimistic about the outcome of their decision.

5. As a group they rationalized away any warning signs.

6. They stereotyped any groups with whom they were in conflict as evil, weak or stupid.

7. They were so convinced of the group's inherent morality that they ignored the ethical and moral implications of their decision.

8. Self-appointed 'mindguards' emerged who took it upon themselves to block incoming information that would contradict the group's beliefs and 'interrupt' the decision-making process.

Janis found that the following groups of policy advisors had been prone to groupthink:

1. Neville Chamberlain's inner circle, whose members supported the policy of appeasement of Hitler during 1937 and 1938, despite repeated warnings and events indicating that it would have adverse consequences.

2. Admiral Kimmel's group of Naval Commanders whose members failed to respond to warnings in the fall of 1941 that Pearl Harbor was in danger of being attacked by Japanese planes.

3. President Truman's advisory group, whose members supported the decision to escalate the war in North Korea despite firm warnings by the Chinese Communist government that United States entry into North Korea would be met with armed resistance from the Chinese.

4. President John F. Kennedy's advisory group, whose members supported the decision to launch the Bay of Pigs invasion of Cuba despite the availability of information indicating that it would be an unsuccessful venture and would damage the United States' relations with other countries.

5. President Lyndon B. Johnson's 'Tuesday luncheon group', whose members supported the decision to escalate the war in Vietnam, despite intelligence reports and other information indicating that this course of action would not defeat the Vietcong or the North Vietnamese

and would entail unfavourable political consequences within the United States.[34]

Signs of groupthink have also been detected in the Watergate cover-up[35] and in Britain's failure to anticipate that Argentina was planning a military invasion of the Falklands.[36]

These are dramatic examples, but there is evidence that much less high-flown groups can show symptoms of groupthink.[37] Which of us has never sat silent through an office meeting in spite of severe anxieties about the way things were going, having decided that the risks of speaking up were too great, that the others might not think you were a 'good colleague', and that anyway 'the group must be right'?

So under what circumstances is groupthink likely to emerge? There are thought to be a combination of factors:

1. The group has no traditions, or no methods, of open-mindedly searching out and evaluating information and alternative options.

2. The group is very tightly knit or 'cohesive',[38] in the jargon, or else they very much *want* to be cohesive;[39] and/or individual members are personally anxious to be accepted by the group.[40]

3. The group is relatively isolated from outside information and expert opinion.

4. The group has a leader who does not promote a spirit of critical inquiry but demands group loyalty and no rocking of the boat.

5. The group is under stress.

The implications for improved decision-making and avoiding the main psychological traps are clear:

1. Get everyone to speak and express doubts, to argue and suggest alternative courses of action, rather than squashing them for doing so.

2. Try to bring out relevant information each person may

have but which the others may not know about, even if it seems to contradict a popular position.

3. Do not indicate that you have a preferred option until everyone else has made their views clear and put their relevant information on the table.

4. Accept criticism of your own judgements.

5. 'Discourage the members from soft-pedaling their disagreements.'[41]

Janis has even suggested that every member of the group should be explicitly asked to act as 'critical evaluators' charged with bringing out doubts and objections; and that a 'devil's advocate' should be appointed to come down hard with counter-arguments to any position that seems to be emerging as the favoured one.

Above all, do not resign yourself to a feeling that office meetings are forever doomed to be tedious time-wasters with unimpressive outcomes. They are not. They *can* be open, productive and cooperative, and they can offer a chance of true participation to your staff instead of being the travesty of consultation or joint decision-making that they so frequently are.

Influence – how to gain it

I just don't know how it happened. One minute I was thinking 'No, I'm not going to cover for Tim at an important client's meeting one more time', and the next minute I hear myself agreeing to do it. I could kick myself.

How am I going to persuade Biggins to let me go on the New York trip? He seems to think I'm too young or incapable of dealing with the cab drivers, or something. There must be a way . . .

It was amazing. Sue and I really turned that meeting around. Perhaps people'll take a bit more notice of me from now on.

Persuasion and influence are an inextricable part of office life. Getting people to change their minds or to agree to something can be quite an art; but if you understand the processes you will be able to resist unpleasant manipulative tactics and to employ the best strategies yourself.

DON'T BE A SUCKER

There are a number of ways people subtly get you to do what they want. Salespeople are often taught them explicitly; naturally persuasive types may hit on them intuitively. However, says American psychologist Robert Cialdini, 'We all employ them and fall victim to them to some degree in our daily interactions with neighbors, friends, lovers, and offspring.' And, he should have added, with the people we work with.

In his book *Influence* he explains why he found this topic so fascinating:

> I can admit it freely now. All my life I've been a patsy. For as long as I can recall, I've been an easy mark for the pitches of peddlers, fund raisers, and operators of one sort or another . . . With personally disquieting frequency, I have always found myself in possession of unwanted magazine subscriptions or tickets to the sanitation workers' ball.

It was his long-standing status as a sucker, he admits, that prompted his interest in what makes people say yes.[1]

There are, he says, a number of persuasive techniques that exploit common human tendencies. Let's look at a few.

The 'foot in the door' technique (FITD)

Perhaps the most famous of all tactics, this involves a small request which is then followed by a large request. It plays on the fact that we like to be consistent in our behaviour and attitudes. Two classic American studies have showed how powerful this sneaky technique can be.

In the first study home-owners were asked by a researcher posing as a volunteer worker to allow a huge, frightful billboard saying 'DRIVE CAREFULLY' to be installed on their front lawns. Not unnaturally, 83 per cent said no.

But in one particular group of people a staggering 76 per cent said yes. About two weeks beforehand, these householders had been asked by another 'volunteer worker' to display a three-inch-square sign in their window saying 'BE A SAFE DRIVER'. Most agreed to this very modest request. But in so doing, psychologists think, they altered their image of themselves to 'I am the kind of person who offers help to people who ask for it.' And they had committed themselves to driver safety. So, in order to be consistent, most of these home-owners then said yes to the huge billboard.

Rather unnervingly, this technique was found to work even

when the first request had little to do with the second one. For example, in the second study, people who agreed to sign a petition to 'keep California beautiful' were much more likely then to agree to the erection of the ghastly 'DRIVE CAREFULLY' sign.[2]

So beware of those trifling requests:

TIM: 'Please would you just watch my briefcase for me while I go to the loo?'

YOU: 'Sure.'

TIM (*returning*): 'Oh, and please could you possibly cover for me at the Kittyfood meeting tomorrow? I've really got to sort out this problem at home.'

YOU: 'Oh, er, all right.'

We may succumb to these pressures because we're not aware of the subtle psychological forces at work. But knowing what factors may be operating does at least give you a chance to resist – or to comply in the full knowledge of what you are doing.

Once you know about FITD you could, of course, use it yourself. However, to avoid a build-up of resentment against you by manipulated colleagues, it might be as well to keep it for dire emergencies. The same applies to the next two tactics as well.

The 'door in the face' technique (DITF)

This is the reverse of the foot-in-the-door strategy: that is, large request first, small request second. Robert Cialdini and his associates have demonstrated how this one works.

They approached unsuspecting college students on campus and brazenly 'asked if they would be willing to chaperon a group of juvenile delinquents on a day trip to the zoo'. All but 17 per cent of the students refused this tempting prospect.

But a different group of students were first asked to 'spend two hours per week as a counsellor to a juvenile delinquent for a minimum of two years'. All of them said no. But then the researchers made the smaller request about the zoo trip – and now 50 per cent of the students agreed.

This happens for two reasons, Cialdini says. First, the retreat from the large request to the small request is seen as a concession. And there is a very strong social rule about reciprocating, whether it be concessions, favours, or other more tangible things.

Second, this technique makes use of the 'contrast principle' – compared to the excessive first request, the second seems relatively minor.[3] (Salespeople often use this to good effect. Having shown you a jacket that costs a horrific £100, they show you another for only £50 and you think it's a snip.)

It might also be, as British social psychologist Steve Duck puts it, that 'We would feel bad about ourselves if we turn the same person down twice in a row. It makes us feel mean or unhelpful.'[4]

You can picture how this might work:

TIM: 'I've got this *tremendous* favour to ask you. Could you possibly cover for me all day tomorrow? This problem at home's really hotting up.'

YOU: 'Oh no, Tim, I really can't. How am I going to manage to do that? What am I going to say? The boss is bound to smell a rat and then we'll both be in the proverbial.'

TIM: 'Yes, of course, I understand. That's fair enough. You couldn't just cover for me at the meeting with Kittyfood in the early afternoon, then, could you?'

YOU (*sighing*): 'Oh, all right, if I must.'

And there you are. Tim's got you again.

The 'low ball' technique

This is a really dirty one. The essence of it is that the villain of the piece offers you inducements to commit yourself to doing something. Then, when you've committed yourself, they backtrack on the incentives. (Or else they will get you to agree to whatever it is in ignorance of the full cost to you, and *then* reveal all.) For example:

TIM: 'If you cover for me at the Kittyfood meeting tomorrow I promise I'll come in early on Saturday morning and let the telephone people in instead of you.'

YOU: 'Oh, OK. Seems fair to me.'

TIM (*later that day*): 'I'm terribly sorry, my wife's just rung, and she's reminded me that I've got to take Amanda to her ballet class first thing on Saturday morning. Sorry, mate – but what can you do?'

Oh dear. Suckered again.

In one study which illustrates the low-ball technique, unsuspecting Iowa residents who heated their homes with natural gas were told that if they were able to reduce the amount of fuel they used during the winter their names would be printed in the newspaper in articles praising public-spirited citizens.

During the next month the residents reduced their gas consumption by over 12 per cent. They were then sent a letter telling them that their names would not after all appear in the paper. It would be natural to expect them to turn the heating up again once the incentive for cutting down had gone. But they didn't; in fact, they cut their consumption even further, by over 15 per cent.[5]

It seems that once a commitment has been made it is often sustained for other reasons even when the initial inducement has disappeared (or the costs of complying have increased). As Robert Cialdini puts it, commitments 'grow their own legs'.[6]

But, as Steve Duck points out, the low-ball technique 'is an extremely offensive and exploitative approach . . . and will lose more friends than it will persuade. Save it for selling cars.'[7]

So watch it, Tim.

How to resist manipulation

The crucial factor in fending off other people's manipulations is *to be aware of what's happening*.

Resisting FITD. On 'slamming the door on the foot-in-the-door', Robert Baron and Donn Byrne say:

> The trick is in paying attention to your own feelings. If you find yourself in a situation where you feel compelled by your former actions to say yes again, pause and ask whether, in the absence of your former compliance [to the initial request], you would be likely to agree now. If the answer is no, then stop right there.[8]

Fending off DITF. Similarly, you can resist the door-in-the-face tactic once you recognize that this is what's going on. You can decide whether or not you want to comply with the second small request *for other reasons* – perhaps you owe the person a favour anyway, perhaps they're having a very bad time at the moment, or whatever. If there are no such reasons, then say no, sorry, to that second request.

'Dodging the low-ball', as Baron and Byrne phrase it:

> If you find yourself in a situation where another person has suddenly altered a prior agreement in a manner that's costly to you, ask yourself the following question: 'Given current conditions, would I have agreed in the first place?' If the answer is no, try to identify the factors that are tempting you to remain in the deal or arrangement. The chances are good you will discover that they are ones of your own creation, and have little or nothing to do with the would-be influencer. At this point, it's probably time to back out.[9]

DIRECT REQUESTS

Much of the time, of course, requests are made directly, as a run-of-the-mill part of everyday life. Bosses have the power to make direct requests of subordinates and just expect them to be complied with. 'Please would you photocopy this for me?' 'I need the finished proposal by noon tomorrow at the latest.'

But with peers and superiors, requests – particularly major ones – are not so straightforward. It is usually best to make sure they're in a good mood first, to elaborate the request with an explanation of why we want whatever it is, and perhaps to offer to do the same for them at some future point. 'Your daughter's just won the school English prize? Well, that's wonderful. Congratulations . . . Oh, George, while I've got you, I have a big favour to ask. Could you *possibly* put up our American visitor for a week instead of me? I know he's a bore and won't eat anything but huge steaks and chews tobacco like some kind of panhandler, but the problem is that my husband's got to have his corrected book proofs at the publishers in ten days' time and he's in such a state that all he does is *snarl* at everyone. What he'd do to Mr Wayne I just dread to think. And Mandy's struggling with exams and forever sobbing down the phone to all her friends about her latest frightful boyfriend. Really, it couldn't be a worse time. If you do this for me, George, I swear I'll stock up on dead cows and spittoons and have the old buzzard to stay the next time he's billeted on you. Oh, thanks, George. You're a hero.'

Simple, really.

Other ways, Steve Duck says, are to 'appeal to the person's good nature,' to give them 'a reminder of a past occasion when the positions were reversed', to make 'a reference to our overwhelming need', or to indicate that their role (as work colleague or superior, say) requires them to help.[10] 'George, you're my closest colleague. Where are we if we can't help each other out in times of crisis?'

The dangers of exploitation

Most people you ask a favour of will be conscious of the need to preserve your relationship – you have to work together, after all. Because of this, within reason they will most likely agree to do as you ask. This is a fact which can, as we've seen, be exploited. Which of us has never been 'put upon' by a colleague or boss, or seen it happen in offices where we have worked?

But this may only be effective for a time. Such exploitation can backfire.

'Psychological reactance'. When a person making a request pushes us *too* hard, we may find ourselves reacting strongly against them and saying no without trouble. There is evidence that when we feel our freedom is being threatened we experience 'psychological reactance' which makes us want to restore our freedom and sense of personal control.[11] So we may take steps to extricate ourselves. In the case of colleagues, perhaps complaining behind their back to people who matter, or finally refusing to comply at a point where the exploiter most needs our acquiescence. 'You've double booked yourself tomorrow with our two most important clients? Sorry, Tim, can't help you out. I've got a meeting myself with the Finnish ambassador on polar bear export licences for our Chocomint ad and there's nothing I can do.' (Oh, the bliss of finally saying no . . .)

In the case of an exploitative boss, we may well find subtle ways of blocking them from getting what they want, or, in the last resort, we may leave the company. None of which will do the boss much good.

So when you next want people you work with to comply with your requests, take into account the fact that you can't just hit and run. They'll be there tomorrow, too.

PERSUADING PEOPLE TO YOUR POINT OF VIEW

Getting people to comply with specific requests is only one aspect of the way we try to influence each other. Now and again, we find ourselves in the position of wanting to *persuade* other people that our point of view on an issue is the correct one. Not just 'Could you write an introduction to this report for me, Martin?' but 'I really think the department should make a push for better catering for client lunches. I thought I'd die when the chef produced boiled cabbage and mince for International Weedkillers' financial director the other day. The guy must've thought he was back at school.'

Sometimes we want to persuade people on an issue where they have no preconceived ideas; more difficult is the situation where they already have a view, and it differs considerably from yours. 'I disagree entirely about the catering. Most successful businessmen have a deep yearning to get away from slivers of underdone carrot shaped like a fan in rich, tarragon sauces. They just want to get back to solid, comforting food that reminds them of nanny.'

But if you really think your position is the right one, what's the best way to put it over?

Roughly speaking, psychologists agree that there are two main ways of convincing others that you're right. People will either focus closely on your arguments, or they will be more affected by peripheral factors such as how they feel about you, what mood they're in, or whether what you're saying is superficially impressive (it contains lots of arguments, say).

Two American psychologists, Richard Petty and John Cacioppo, have called these the 'central route' and the 'peripheral route' to persuasion.[12] Both can operate at the same time.[13]

The 'central route' to persuasion

With the central route, people think carefully about the positions you have proposed to them. If they find your arguments cogent and compelling, they will develop favourable thoughts in their minds about your views, and their attitudes will shift in your direction. 'If,' on the other hand, 'the arguments are found to be weak and specious, they will be counterargued and the message will be resisted – or boomerang (change opposite to that intended) may even occur.'[14]

But how do you judge the most effective route to persuading others? When will the strength of your arguments be the crucial factor, and when will extraneous matters such as the other person's mood and their attitudes towards you be more important?

The most obvious indicator is how much the issue matters to them. The more it matters, the more they're going to analyse your arguments and – if they don't initially share your views – they'll think up arguments against you as much as they can. So your arguments have *got* to be good.

You have to work out what the other person needs and values, and where their interests lie; then you have to show how what you want them to do will benefit them. 'If we start serving French low-fat cuisine to clients, that will give exactly the stylish image you've been working towards. It'll just reinforce the impression made by all that designer office furniture we've been perching on for the last year.'

But do you only present arguments in favour of your position, or do you take the bull by the horns by including arguments against your position and then refute them?

The evidence is that when everybody is pretty much on your side anyway, 'one-sided' arguments are fine. But when everyone is against you it's better to produce 'two-sided' arguments in which you acknowledge and rebut their position.[15] 'I know that some clients long for nursery food, but they can get that at places other than here and it just doesn't gel with the strong, progressive image we're trying to create. They might *enjoy* suet pudding and custard, but will it increase their respect for us?'

If your arguments are in fact pretty complicated, it'll be more effective to present them in writing to begin with so that people can take them in properly.[16] Then you can go and push the points home with a face-to-face presentation.

And, the evidence is, the more arguments you provide, the better. Petty and Cacioppo have found that by increasing the number of arguments you can affect how easily persuaded people are *whether or not* they are motivated to scrutinize their contents.[17] If they are sufficiently involved in the issue to analyse your arguments, then they are more likely to find at least one of them convincing. If they are not involved, they may just be impressed by the sheer number of arguments and reckon there must be something in it, and so will be more likely to go along with you.

The 'peripheral route'

People aren't always sufficiently motivated or able to consider carefully the position you're putting forward, however. Your colleague Mr Wimpheart, for example, may never be lucky enough to take clients to meals, and therefore won't feel terribly strongly about the lunchtime catering. But you may need unanimity to push your ideas through; and people can change their attitudes even when they don't diligently assess the pros and cons of the matter.

The way this happens, Petty and Cacioppo suggest, is via the 'peripheral route'. Here, attitudes change because of superficial factors or 'cues' that are unrelated to the actual content of your case.

Putting the other in a good mood. One positive factor is the *mood* someone is in at the time you're trying to persuade them. You have to make sure that you don't catch them in a bad mood and, ideally, you should wait until they're in a good one. You can create a warm and pleasant atmosphere yourself; humour, for example, is an excellent way of doing this.

Henry Kissinger, it is said, used humour to ease his

negotiations with world leaders, and there is some evidence that his instincts were sound. R. Valeriani, an expert on Kissinger and author of *Travels with Henry*, commented on the Russian–American negotiations: 'Neither side changed its basic policy because of the levity . . . but the humor relaxed the atmosphere and created a more propitious climate for making accommodations.'[18]

Two social psychologists, Karen O'Quin and Joel Aronoff, did a rather artificial but nonetheless interesting demonstration of the value of humour. They had 252 male and female American undergraduates take part in simulated negotiations over the price of a landscape painting. Each subject played the 'buyer' and bargained with a confederate of the experimenter who played the 'seller'. The latter started with an asking price of $70,000, and the subject was told to start at $25,000. When the bargainers had bid to within about $10,000 of each other, the confederate said either 'Well, my final offer is X dollars,' or, smiling, 'Well, my final offer is X dollars, and I'll throw in my pet frog.'

As the experimenters hoped, subjects exposed to this sally did actually find it funny. And, as predicted, they made greater concessions to their opponent immediately after hearing it than did the unamused subjects who hadn't been offered the frog.

But why did it happen? Subjects generally liked their opponents and the joke didn't increase their liking further. The researchers think the humour may have put the subjects in a better mood, or that joking led them to redefine the negotiations as less important or threatening than they had thought, making concessions easier.[19]

It's worth a go, anyway, but do try to think of something better than the pet frog, for heaven's sake . . .

Another way of relaxing the atmosphere is the notorious 'business lunch'. 'Let's lush up old Catacomb, and he's bound to swing the deal our way.' What is less generally realized is that this is only likely to be a powerful technique if Catacomb is *already* on your side and just needs a small push, or if it's a deal of only minor importance to him. Otherwise it'll be your arguments that matter, not the deliciousness of the profiteroles and the vintage of the claret.

Your credibility. Probably more important than the other's mood is how credible you are personally: how competent you appear to be, how interested and enthusiastic you are, how attractive they find you as a person, how trustworthy you seem, and so on. Trustworthiness is often judged by whether or not you have an 'axe to grind'; if you have, you may sound rather less convincing than you would otherwise.[20] 'Yes, my sister has just finished her chef's training, and is going to specialize in business lunches. Not that that affects my views of our current chef, of course . . .'

It's important to make sure you appear to have the 'right' motives – that you clearly take others' interests into account and not just your own. 'Well, I don't care personally if clients get a bit of stale bread and a spot of flat mineral water for lunch; but Jan's a good sort and definitely on the ball, so if she thinks our catering is a pig's breakfast I suspect she's probably right.'

Psychologists aren't sure whether credibility simply acts as a cue – 'This person knows what they're talking about/I like them/I trust them, so what they're saying must be OK' – or whether it makes people focus more on what you're saying.[21] It may sometimes be one, sometimes the other, so you shouldn't just rely on your credibility and assume everyone thinks you're so wonderful that you can get away with weak arguments.

Style of presentation. The way you present your case can also be a peripheral persuader. As Robert Baron puts it:

Persons who present their message in a fluent, convincing style tend to be more persuasive than ones who stumble over their words, or who show signs of low self-confidence. Interestingly, considerable evidence suggests that communicators who speak at a faster-than-average pace are actually more persuasive than ones who present their messages more slowly.[22]

Essentially, you've got to sound confident and appear to know what you're talking about.

Rules of thumb. If people aren't going to take the time to think the matter over terribly carefully, they're likely to rely on mental 'rules of thumb' – how many arguments there are, how much expertise the persuader appears to have, and such things as whether the argument is bolstered by statistics. 'Well, research shows that 78 per cent of high-income businessmen prefer light lunches – raw carrot wins over spotted dick.'

These operate as 'persuasion cues': 'plenty of arguments, conclusion probably correct'; 'experts usually know their stuff'; 'statistics, hey, must be right'.[23]

Overall, the peripheral route is just what it sounds like. As Petty and Cacioppo put it:

> Rather than carefully evaluating the issue-relevant arguments, a person may accept an advocacy simply because it is presented during a pleasant lunch or because the message source is an expert. Similarly, a person may reject an advocacy simply because the position presented appears to be too extreme or because the source is unattractive.[24]

Cover your options

If you've done your best as regards your own credibility, the general emotional ambience at the time you make your persuasion attempt, and the number of arguments you can produce, then you have increased your chances of persuading the other via the peripheral route. That is, in circumstances where the person is not motivated or is unable to focus closely on the content of your arguments. And obviously, even when they are going to beam in on the quality of your case, these factors will do no harm and may even help things along.

On top of that, as it is not always easy to judge how the other is going to respond, you've just got to try to make your arguments as strong as possible. And if you think you're going to have a real struggle to persuade them to your point of view, remember to include rebuttals of arguments you think they are going to come up with.

And go for it.

INFLUENCING A GROUP

Obviously, the above considerations apply whether you're trying to persuade one person or several. But when you're a member of a group, additional factors come into play. As we saw in the last chapter, there are strong pressures towards conformity with what appears to be the group's overall opinion. At your department's weekly meeting, say, if everyone else seems rather keen on recruiting a new accountant whom you feel is completely unsuitable, and probably qualified by correspondence course from Reading jail, what do you do?

Psychologists find that there are two main reasons why we feel strong pressures to conform to a group consensus. First, we want to be liked and accepted by the other members. Second, we like to be right.[25] And if everyone else thinks that Messrs Twist, Bentworthy and Corkscrew are the ideal choice of accountant, well, isn't the group always right?

But, as we know, the group isn't always right. And if you think that you are, then how can you persuade the others?

The influence of minorities

Just because you are in the minority it doesn't mean you should throw up your hands in despair. There is plenty of evidence in life that minorities can influence majorities; and the French social psychologist Serge Moscovici and his associates, in particular, have done a lot of research on the factors which make them most likely to succeed.[26] The most important are:

1. When the minority is consistent in its position over time and doesn't keep wobbling about, sometimes agreeing with the majority and sometimes not.
2. When the minority is in agreement internally – it presents a united front.
3. When the minority does not appear too extreme, rigid or dogmatic. The majority are likely just to reject their views out of hand, without consideration.

The point is that the majority should be made to see that the minority are espousing this position not because they are dogmatic by nature, or solely concerned with narrow self-interest, but because they are convinced, confident and committed enough to stand up against the group. In other words, it must be the strength of the position itself that is causing the minority to stick out for it. This provides your best chance of shaking up the majority and making them rethink the whole issue. It may either shift them towards your position or perhaps lead them to come up with a new solution altogether.[27]

If you have recruited any allies, make sure you are in total agreement so as not to undermine the strength of your arguments. Make it clear, too, that you can see the merits in the others' position, but you still feel your suggestion is a better option. 'Of course, I agree that Messrs Twist, Bentworthy and Corkscrew *are* a successful thorn in the side of the Inland Revenue. What concerns me is the other side of the coin; their methods cause sharp intakes of breath when their name comes up over the port at the accountants' association annual dinner. Given that the government has just given us a lucrative new contract, is this connection going to be quite wise, d'you think?'

Even if you have no allies, if you're not known as a particularly dogmatic or narrow-minded person, you may be just as effective as if you have. Why, the group will ask themselves, would you be holding out for a minority position if there weren't something in it?[28] Your personal standing is therefore something to consider. There is evidence that in a group you can earn 'idiosyncrasy credits' for yourself.[29] That is, if your group feels that you are a loyal member with the interests of the group at heart, that you are sufficiently competent to have furthered those interests in the past, and that you have gone along with the group on previous occasions, then you have probably built up enough credit with them to be occasionally idiosyncratic and disagree with them without being rejected. 'Well, if *Sally* thinks we're all wrong about moving our creative department to a flotilla of linked barges under Tower Bridge, maybe she's got a point . . .'

Being seen as influential

Trying to convert a majority who are against you is, of course, the hardest persuasive task you'll ever have to do in a group. In general, we just want to contribute to the discussions and have the others take notice of our views. What *is* it, then, that makes other people regard one as an influential group member?

On top of obvious factors such as your position in the organization, two things that seem to be very important are 'air time' – how much you talk – and, not surprisingly, the quality or accuracy of what you say. But which is the more vital in determining how influential you are?

Preston Bottger of the University of New South Wales has made a study of the difference between how influential people are *seen* to be from how influential they *actually* are.[30] He got middle-level managers and graduate management students to tackle a complex problem, in groups of four to six members.

The problem chosen was the 'NASA moon survival test', which is very commonly used in psychological research on decision-making. The participants were to imagine they were members of a space crew which had crash-landed on the light side of the moon 200 miles from their rendezvous point with the mother ship. They had to rank the fifteen items of equipment left undamaged in the crash in order of their importance in enabling the crew to reach the mother ship alive. The most critical item would be ranked 1, the least critical, 15. For interest, the items and correct rankings were:

NASA MOON SURVIVAL TEST[31]

Equipment	Correct ranking	Reason
Box of matches	15	Useless since there is no oxygen on the moon
Food concentrate	4	Satisfies basic energy requirements
50 feet of nylon rope	6	Useful in scaling cliffs, tying injured together, etc.
Parachute silk	8	Protection from sun's rays
Portable heating unit	13	Only useful if on the dark side of the moon
Two .45 calibre pistols	11	Possible source of self-propulsion
1 case dehydrated Pet milk	12	Duplicates food concentrate in bulkier form
2 hundred-pound tanks of oxygen	1	Absolute necessity for life support
Stellar map (of the moon's constellation)	3	Most important means of determining position and directions
Life raft	9	CO_2 bottle possible propulsion device
Magnetic compass	14	Virtually useless since magnetic field on the moon isn't polarized
5 gallons of water	2	Absolute necessity to sustain life
Signal flares	10	Possible distress signal once close enough to mother ship to be seen

Equipment	Correct ranking	Reason
First aid kit containing injection needles	7	Injection needles fitted to suit aperture quite useful
Solar-powered FM receiver-transmitter	5	Only useful if line-of-sight transmission is possible with limited transmission range

Each participant was first asked to work on the problem alone in order to give a rating of their individual expertise. The closer their answers to the correct ones above, which had been provided by NASA personnel, the greater their expertise was assumed to be.

The participants were then told to reach a team solution to the problem. Afterwards, each participant was asked to rate how influential they thought the other team members had been in reaching the solution.

In order to assess their actual influence, the group's answers were compared with each member's initial answers. The closer the match, the greater the member's influence was assumed to have been. Meanwhile two independent observers listened to tape recordings of the sessions to get a measure of each member's 'air time'.

The results of Bottger's study implied that how influential you are *seen* to be is more a function of 'air time' than of expertise, and your *actual* influence is determined more by your expertise than by how much you participate.

To enhance your reputation as an influential person, then, it is important to contribute as much as you can in terms of quantity to the discussions (without driving everyone else insane by hogging the floor the entire time, of course). But to have real influence you need to make sure you've done your homework and know what you're talking about. Quantity alone won't see you through unscathed. On the basis of his observations of real groups Bottger says: 'An individual with a reputation for high-quantity/low-quality contributions tends to be disregarded and discouraged.' So talk a lot – but talk sense . . .

Women in mixed-sex groups

Psychologists have often found what many women, to their cost, know to be true: that men frequently dominate in group discussions where both men and women are present. It appears to be less likely to happen when women are known to be – and feel themselves to be – competent in the area under discussion.[32] As we have already seen, it is vital to be self-confident, assertive and knowledgeable. '*My* feeling is that our best plan would be to shelve the gerbil licensing campaign altogether. Frankly, no one will pay the fee, and it'll just mean hundreds of newly homeless gerbils roaming the streets in little furry gangs. Remember what happened when they tried it in Sweden . . .'

Don't be overwhelmed

Trying to be persuasive and influential in a group setting may seem more daunting than when you've just got one person to deal with. The important thing is not to feel overwhelmed. Remember that you have credit with the group as a credible, competent, loyal person. So if you've got something to say, say it. Sound confident, don't put anyone else down, recruit allies beforehand if necessary. You won't always get your way, of course, but at least you may influence the final group decision. And further enhance your reputation, to boot.

Stress – how to beat it

When I crawl out of bed in the mornings, I can feel myself tensing up like a clock spring. I think about my Eiffel-tower-sized in-tray, the boss's scowling face, the next deadline. It's ghastly.

I feel sick to my stomach before every single meeting. My head feels like it's gripped in a steel vice, and it takes every ounce of willpower to get myself in there and not to start gibbering.

I get to the stage where I think 'If that phone rings just one more time, I'm going to pick it up and yell obscenities into it.' It never seems to stop. I can't stand it.

Sound familiar? If you've ever felt like that, you were in the throes of a nasty dose of stress. 'Stress' is one of the buzzwords of the late twentieth century. We're all either suffering from it, have suffered from it, know a lot of people who have, or expect to feel it any minute.

How common is stress? If you're currently feeling stressed, join the throng. The British National Survey of Health and Development found that 42 per cent of twenty-six-year-old female respondents who were working full-time reported being under 'some' or 'severe' nervous strain at work. Of the thirty-two-year-olds, 46 per cent said so. For men the figures were 40 and 44 per cent respectively.[1]

But for most of us, stress is probably spasmodic rather than chronic. Two psychologists from the University of Sheffield, Peter Warr and Roy Payne, asked random samples of 1162 men and 181 women in full-time employment whether they had experienced any 'unpleasant emotional strain' on the previous day. They defined this as 'any *unpleasant* feelings of being upset, distressed, worried, anxious, harassed, angry, depressed, sad, and so on'.

Of the men, 15 per cent said they had experienced such strain and attributed it to their job; of these, 4 per cent said they had felt that way for half or more of the day. The corresponding figures for women were 10 and 3 per cent.[2]

Putting the survey findings together, it's clear that feelings of stress typically come and go – or, for the lucky ones, may rarely come at all.

What is stress? It's important to realize that having heaped in-trays, constantly ringing telephones and moody bosses does not automatically mean that you are under stress. People vary a great deal in their susceptibility to stress,[3] and demands that would have one person screaming for mercy and fleeing for the exit would have another rubbing their hands and excitedly getting stuck in. It's not so much *what* happens to you, it's how you react to it that matters.

There's a lot of argument about the exact definition of stress. Very crudely, it's 'the strain a person experiences from the pressure of outside forces',[4] and is typically identified in terms of its adverse effects.

THE EFFECTS OF STRESS

Demands made upon us that can cause stress – called 'stressors' – are usually present to a greater or lesser degree. As one of the first scientists to work on stress-related illness, Hans Selye, put it, 'Complete freedom from stress only comes with death!'[5]

Low to moderate levels of stress can be stimulating. It's when the stress becomes too high – and, in particular, too prolonged – that problems set in.[6]

Physical effects

Prolonged stress, by upsetting our body chemistry and other bodily responses, can lead to – or lower our resistance to – disease and illness.[7] Rather alarmingly, it has been estimated that 50 to 70 per cent of all physical illness is at least partly caused by stress.[8]

Stress-related illnesses include:

high blood pressure
heart disease
stomach ulcers
diabetes
asthma
rheumatoid arthritis[9]

There are other physical problems which could be warning signals. For example:

headaches
migraines
appetite changes
nausea
diarrhoea/constipation
dizziness
eczema[10]

A horrid collection of complaints altogether.

Stress expert Professor Cary Cooper of the University of Manchester Institute of Science and Technology, and his colleague Marilyn Davidson, have done an in-depth study of sixty women managers. Quotes from these women bring the problems vividly alive:

> I get frequent upset stomachs which I know are directly related to my job. Indeed, as soon as I know I have to see my boss about something, I find it hard to cope and feel my stomach grip.

> My job has given me severe headaches and frequently

crying bouts. I also find it very difficult to sleep before a big meeting or when I feel I'm being evaluated.

Bodily protests against excessive stress may be less frequent than psychological ones.

Psychological effects

In their study, Cooper and Davidson found far higher rates of psychological than of physical stress-related symptoms. This is their list of psychological symptoms:

> anger
> irritation
> anxiety
> tiredness
> low self-esteem
> depression
> tension (neck or back)
> sleeplessness
> frustration
> dissatisfaction with life or job[11]

Other signs include indecisiveness, lack of concentration and loss of libido.[12]

Stress can influence how well you do your job, and strongly affect your personal life. In counterproductive attempts to cope, many people start relying on tobacco, alcohol or drugs.[13] Not at all a good idea.

One of Cooper and Davidson's subjects, for example:

> When I first became a supervisor I smoked more and sometimes I would come home and bawl my eyes out. I used to say to my husband that it's too much, I can't cope. I still feel the pressure and the symptoms still occur but less frequently and less severely.[14]

Failing to cope successfully with prolonged, intense stress can lead to 'burnout'. Victims of burnout 'become exhausted (both emotionally and physically), grow cynical, and develop negative attitudes toward their work, other persons, and life in general'.[15]

'**Feeling bad**'. Essentially, a degree of stress is an inescapable part of life and is usually fine. It only becomes a problem when it starts to make you feel grim. You may not at first even be very conscious of the danger; you might not realize what those persistent headaches and outbursts of temper are all about. 'Snebbings, for God's sake, how many goddamn times do I have to tell you not to walk past my desk like that?' Bad sign, bad sign.

If you think you are suffering from a selection of the psychological symptoms listed above, it's vital to try to think seriously about what might be causing them so that you can then take action quickly. Otherwise, not only will the quality of your life be seriously impaired, but you will risk making yourself ill.

If you have already noticed a downturn in your physical health, it's essential to go to your doctor. You must tell your doctor about any extreme pressures in your work or personal life, and this will help him or her to form an opinion.

Doctors sometimes prescribe tranquillizers, antidepressants or sleeping pills, and more people use them than is commonly realized. Cary Cooper and his associates have found that in samples of British senior executives, about 30 per cent of the men and over 40 per cent of the women had been or were currently taking stress-relieving drugs.[16] (The women's rates were probably higher for a number of reasons: the pressure of coping with work as well as keeping a home, dealing with discrimination at work, etc.)

Such drugs may help you over the worst, but they do not tackle the root of the problem, and should *not* be relied on long-term. It's that root cause that needs to be dealt with.

CAUSES OF STRESS

Obviously, plenty of things can cause stress.[17] A few of the most common ones are:

1. *Work overload.* Either you've got too much to do and too little time to do it in, or else the job is very difficult and complex and you're constantly on the verge of feeling that you can't handle it. Or both. 'Oh. You want the five-year plan by three o'clock, and a resolution of that tricky policy problem by four? And our chief sponsor's on the phone wanting a long chat? Oh fine. Absolutely fine.' Pause. '*Aaaargh!*' Know the feeling?

2. *Poor relationships with bosses, colleagues or subordinates.* 'The boss is always so *off-hand*. It doesn't matter how hard I try, I never get any praise.' 'Jim's always so wretchedly snide. And I've got to work with him, it's really getting to me.'

3. *Lack of autonomy.* Having no control over your job, and no participation in decision-making that affects it, is thought to be one of the main sources of stress. 'My boss is so damned *autocratic*. I don't get any say in anything.'

4. *Role ambiguity.* This means that it's not clear what you're expected to achieve in your job, what your boss and colleagues expect of you, what the scope and responsibility of the job is, and so on. 'I don't really know what she wants of me.' 'I'm not sure if that's my responsibility or Jane's – I miscalculated something rotten last week, and she was shirty with me for ages, claiming I was treading on her toes.'

5. *Role conflict.* Sometimes you find yourself caught between conflicting demands – from your boss and your subordinates, say – and that can be stressful.

One particularly difficult conflict can arise between your work role and your role as spouse or family person. 'Yes, I know I've been working till ten o'clock every night to finish that report and haven't told Susie a bedtime story for three weeks. But what can I do?'

What to do? There are many other factors too, but endless lists aren't terribly helpful. What may be a stressor for one person may not be for another. The important issue is what *you* find stressful.

You may, of course, be lucky enough to work in a company that employs a stress counsellor or offers stress management courses – but it's unlikely. Britain lags woefully behind, say, the United States in these respects. According to Cary Cooper, stress-related illnesses are declining in America because – unlike Britain – companies have to insure their employees' health, so they put a lot of effort into making sure they stay well. 'In Britain, employers don't pay the cost of bad management, the National Health Service does.'[18] Even so, Cary Cooper says, 'They should see the "cost saving" argument in terms of lost work days, absenteeism, poor performance, premature death, retraining, etc.'[19]

If you are constantly feeling in a really terrible state, and your company won't do anything useful, it might be best to seek some outside help. Psychotherapy can be very effective with people who are suffering very severely from job-related distress.[20]

If it's not yet as bad as that, but you're not feeling too good, let's see what you can do for yourself.

WAYS OF COPING

Sad to say, there are no magic formulas of the 'If I picture a tub of petunias every time the boss shouts at me I'll be OK' variety. Psychologists have only quite recently begun to study the question of which of the many strategies that people use to cope with stress are most likely to work; and results are not always consistent.[21] ('Coping' here refers to the attempt to deal with a stressor, whether or not it actually succeeds.) Clearly, whether any particular tactic to cope with stress will do the trick or not depends on lots of factors, such as 'the demands and constraints of the context in which it is being used and the skill with which it is applied'.[22] But evidence is accumulating that *acting* to do something about the stressor itself is generally a good idea; avoiding the whole issue is not.

Problem-focused coping

One of the relatively few studies to look specifically at how coping strategies affect job stress was done by Janina Latack of Ohio State University. She gave questionnaires to managers and professionals in a medium-sized manufacturing firm and in an osteopathic hospital. They were asked to think how frequently they react in a given way in three specific types of situation: role ambiguity, role conflict and role overload. These are three of the most common stressors. Role ambiguity, for example, was described as being 'uncertain of what you are supposed to do on your job or unsure of how to approach a particular assignment'.

What Latack found was that a certain group of coping strategies, which she labelled 'control strategies', looked promising. 'Individuals adopting a control strategy are less likely to report job-related anxiety, job dissatisfaction and to leave the organization.'

Her list of control strategies is as follows:

1. Get together with my supervisor to discuss this.
2. Try to be very organized so that I can keep on top of things.
3. Talk with people (other than my supervisor) who are involved.
4. Try to see this situation as an opportunity to learn and develop new skills.

5. Put extra attention on planning and scheduling.

6. Try to think of myself as a winner – as someone who always comes through.

7. Tell myself that I can probably work things out to my advantage.

8. Devote more time and energy to doing my job.

9. Try to get additional people involved in the situation.

10. Think about the challenges I can find in this situation.

11. Try to work faster and more efficiently.

12. Decide what I think should be done and explain this to the people who are affected.

13. Give it my best effort to do what I think is expected of me.

14. Request help from people who have the power to do something for me.

15. Seek advice from people outside the situation who may not have power but who can help me think of ways to do what is expected of me.

16. Work on changing policies which caused this situation.

17. Throw myself into my work and work harder, longer hours.[23]

Latack lumped all these strategies together, and of course it's quite likely that some will be generally more effective than others, and some will work in certain situations and not in others. Working harder, for instance, may only serve to decrease stress if it's just a short burst to get rid of an anxiety-making demand, or if the stressful situation has built up because you've been slacking and spending too much time down the pizza parlour at lunchtime. But what these strategies have in common is the attempt to *get to grips* with what's happening.

It's possible that, since these strategies were only *linked* with lower stress in Latack's study (rather than been proved definitely to cause lower stress), less stressed people may simply be more likely to use control strategies. But the notion that getting to grips with the problem can help fits with other studies of stress that aren't confined to the work-place; for example, those that ask random samples of the population to think about a recent stressful event and how they reacted to it.

In several such studies, people who were able to resolve stressful situations satisfactorily[24] and who suffered less psychological damage[25] were found to be more likely to have used a 'planful problem-solving' approach. This was measured by questionnaire items such as:

1. I knew what had to be done, so I doubled my efforts to make things work.
2. I made a plan of action and followed it.
3. I just concentrated on what I had to do next – the next step.
4. I changed something so things would turn out all right.
5. I drew on my past experiences; I was in a similar position before.
6. I came up with a couple of different solutions to the problem.[26]

Certain personality traits seem to make people more resistant to stress, and this may be because people who have them are more prone to using coping strategies that are likely to be effective. For example:

'Hardiness'. An American psychologist, Suzanne Kobasa, and her colleagues have found evidence that a particular grouping of personality characteristics – which they call 'hardiness' – helps people to stave off the damaging effects of stress. These characteristics are: 'commitment, control and challenge'.[27]

Essentially, hardy people tend to *involve* themselves in what's going on, rather than feeling alienated from it; they feel and act as though they are *influential* (rather than helpless) in the face of the ups and downs of life; and they see life as a challenge. 'The challenge disposition is expressed as the belief that change rather than stability is normal in life and that the anticipation of changes are interesting incentives to growth rather than threats to security.'[28]

Seeing something as challenging makes problem-focused coping, positive thinking and good morale more likely; viewing it as a threat is distressing, and may reduce the chances of coming to grips with it.[29] 'The MD's on the warpath again, is he? Just smashed his favourite executive toy in a fit of temper and heading in this direction, flame darting from his nostrils? No problem. If I don't have him cooing like a turtle dove in under ten minutes, the lunchtime bottle of Perrier's on me.'

Optimism. Optimists tend to be more resistant to stress than pessimists, and the evidence is that they tend to use different types of coping strategies. American psychologist Michael Scheier and his colleagues have discovered that optimists are more likely to use problem-focused coping such as the 'planful problem-solving' strategies above, and similar ones such as taking action quickly before things get out of hand.

They also found that optimists tend more than pessimists to seek *social support*. For example, optimists will talk to someone else about how they are feeling, or ask someone they respect for advice and follow it.[30] Several of Latack's 'control strategies', too, involved seeking out other people at stressful times; and there's plenty of evidence from other sources that having social support can relieve the effects of stress.[31]

Good relationships with your boss and colleagues can be especially helpful; they can provide not only emotional support, but also relevant information and ideas.[32] 'God, Bob, I've just got to tell you – the boss is really livid because I took our top Muslim client to a restaurant called The Stuffed Pig. What do you think she'll do to me? Oh, hey, that's a good idea. Tell her that it does the best saffron rice in town? It's worth a try . . .'

There can, however, be a danger in social support if it actually prevents you from doing what you can to tackle the stressful problem itself. Suzanne Kobasa and her colleague, Mark Puccetti, studied executives under pressure from stressful events. Those who were not 'hardy' and who had a lot of family support showed more stress symptoms. 'At a time when their jobs were requiring discipline and task-orientation, low hardiness executives may be unfortunately encouraged by their families to allow themselves some self-pity and the distraction of a preoccupation with how they feel.'[33] As a result, they may not try to resolve their work difficulties. They need less of the brow-stroking, 'Have a good moan, darling' approach and more of the 'Have you tried talking to Richard about it?' tack.

Optimists – as you'd expect! – tend more to *emphasize the positive* aspects of the stressful situation. They're more likely to say that, for example, they 'changed or grew as a person in a new way' or 'found new faith or some important truth about life'.

Another strategy Scheier and his associates found in optimists more than in pessimists was *'acceptance/resignation'* – but only when the situation was seen as uncontrollable. For example, optimists 'accepted it, since nothing could be done', or they 'made light of the situation, refused to get too serious about it'. This 'resigned' approach would almost certainly be of use when indeed you couldn't actually do anything to alter the situation.[34] But it could be counterproductive if it stopped you acting to improve matters when the situation was, in fact, at least partly under your control.

Humour. Making light of it all, of course, doesn't necessarily mean you won't do something about it. And if you can manage it, it could well help. The biblical maxim that 'a merry heart doeth good like a medicine' is supported by evidence that people with a strong sense of humour, who use it as a way of dealing with stressful experiences, are less vulnerable to stress.[35] 'Steve's been in such a bad mood with me for days, I'm going to have to talk to him about it. But I have to tell you – the way his ears waggle as he's gearing up for a really blistering attack, like an adolescent duck preparing for take-off, just cracks me up. I keep having to dash to the gents and muffle my laughter in the roller towel.'

Feeling in control. The general theme emerging from this research is clear: it's usually best to try to exert some control over the situation rather than collapsing in a helpless heap. Indeed, there is evidence that people who have an 'internal locus of control' – that is, they feel their life is under their own control – are generally less vulnerable to stress than those with an 'external locus of control', who think they are at the mercy of fate and outside circumstances.[36]

Problem-focused strategies might, however, make you feel worse when the situation is, *in reality*, out of your control.[37] In such circumstances, the evidence is that what they say about positive thinking is all true: people who find something positive in awful, uncontrollable events show less distress than those who don't.[38] 'Well, I suppose the fact that my major client has just gone into liquidation means I don't have to sit across conference tables from that revolting, sarcastic, ego-slashing managing director of theirs one more time ... And I used to *hate* the way he'd stick his biro in his ear and rotate it like an electric drill. Used to make me feel quite poorly.'

Of course, positive thinking is also a good idea when you *can* do something about what's happened. Latack counts it as a 'control strategy', and it may help you to confront the problem. 'I'm terrific at rush jobs. I always think I can't do it

– yet I've never missed a deadline yet. OK, so I've got to analyse possible links between not buying Wheetiflakes' Sugarfree Vitabran and rising crime rates in Greater London by lunchtime and it's 10.30 now. I can do it, don't panic. And afterwards, I'm going to tell the boss I'd like more notice in future . . .'

What not to do

Trying to do something specific about the stressor seems to be more effective than certain other types of reaction, particularly trying to escape or evade the issue – what you might call the 'head under the duvet' syndrome.

In Janina Latack's study, the use of what she called 'escape strategies' was associated with psychosomatic complaints like pains in the back or spine and sleeplessness. These strategies include:

1. Avoiding being in this situation if you can.
2. Telling yourself that time takes care of situations like this.
3. Reminding yourself that work isn't everything.
4. Separating yourself as much as possible from the people who created the situation.
5. Trying not to get concerned about it.
6. Accepting the situation because there is nothing you can do to change it.
7. Setting your own priorities based on what you like to do.[39]

As with control strategies, to lump the escape strategies together like this disguises the possible subtleties. Reminding yourself that work isn't everything seems like a splendid idea to me as a way of lessening your distress a bit, but not if it actually stops you from tackling the problem and getting rid of it properly. Then again, if the problem is really not under your control, then number 6 above is not such a bad tactic.

But the general principle that avoiding matters won't, on the whole, diminish your stress – and may even exacerbate it – is supported by other research, too. Suzanne Kobasa, for example, found in a sample of lawyers under stress that those who tried to deny, minimize or get away from stressful situations showed more psychological and physical symptoms of strain.[40]

In another study, 'escapist' strategies were found to *increase* emotional distress after a stressful episode. 'Escapism' consisted of:

1. Having fantasies or wishes about how things might turn out.
2. Daydreaming or imagining a better time or place than the one you are in.
3. Wishing that the situation would go away or somehow be over with.
4. Thinking about fantastic or unreal things (like the perfect revenge or finding a million dollars) that make you feel better.
5. Avoiding being with people in general.
6. Trying to make yourself feel better by eating, drinking, smoking, using drugs or medication, etc.
7. Sleeping more than usual.[41]

The danger with fantasizing and daydreaming and so on – jolly as it is – may be that, although it makes you feel better temporarily, the cause of the stress is still lurking untouched. And so the stress can build up . . .

Michael Scheier and his colleagues also pointed to the disadvantages of escapism. They discovered that pessimists, who are less successful than optimists at dealing with stress, are more prone to 'denial and distancing': for example, they 'refused to believe that it had happened' and 'tried to forget the whole thing'. Pessimists are also inclined to focus on and express their stressful feelings. 'Stone the crows, do I feel the *pits*. I'm so miserable, my head hurts, my stomach feels like I've been kicked by a horse, I'm as taut as stretched elastic.' It can of course help to tell other people about your ghastly state – it's good to let it out somehow – but don't make a habit of dwelling on the nasty feelings as such. It isn't a productive tactic. It may make you feel even more pessimistic and sorry for yourself and hold you back from tackling the source of the stress.

Take action

If you're feeling stressed, you need to try to analyse precisely what it is about your working life that makes you feel you're about to explode or crumble, and direct your efforts into doing something about it. Cast your mind back to the moments when you felt it was all too much. What was happening then? What are the types of events that consistently wind you up? Make a list if it helps you to clarify things.

When you have done this, it may then be perfectly clear what you need to do. Leave this particular job (maybe even get a different type of job), ask for a transfer, try to get the company to reduce the stressor if it lies within their control, be more assertive if people are piling unfair amounts of work on to you, ask for a precise definition of your job responsibilities, or whatever.

However, direct action to remove or minimize the stressor may not always be possible. If that is the case, you may find 'stress management techniques' useful, and the rest of this chapter is devoted to looking at some of these.

STRESS MANAGEMENT TECHNIQUES

Bookshops are usually heaving with piles of books on how to manage stress. The most popular techniques are those which people can use all the time and which act as a protection against the possibly damaging effects of a stressful life.

Relaxation

Running around like a hare with its ears on fire from morning till night is not a great idea. If you can take some time out each day to relax and gather your strength you will really feel the benefit, since relaxation reduces the impact of stressors on your physical and psychological health.[42]

There are a number of different relaxation methods[43] to choose from. Here's one to give you a flavour. It combines elements of meditation, visualization and 'progressive muscle relaxation':

1. *Find a quiet place* where you will not be interrupted. (Remember to take the phone off the hook.)

2. *Close your eyes and relax.* Slowly take three deep breaths and visualize each part of your body relaxing progressively from your toes to your head.

3. *Count down slowly* from 10 to 1. Visualize yourself descending to your meditative state of mind, which can be achieved by seeing yourself in a peaceful scene from nature, a hideaway room, or any comfortable place you like.

4. *Slowly repeat the word 'one'* in your mind. When other thoughts come in, let them pass and gently return to repeating the word *one*. It is important to avoid straining to concentrate.

5. *Count yourself back up* from 1 to 10 and say to yourself that you will awake refreshed, relaxed, and in a positive frame of mind.[44]

Do this for ten to twenty minutes if you can; otherwise whatever you can manage. You may open your eyes to glance at the time. An alarm is not recommended – it could give you a terrific shock. When you're in the depths of a meditative state, an alarm bell can sound like a gas explosion. And give yourself a few minutes before getting up.

Emergencies. You might also need an emergency technique, a slightly more sophisticated version of the famous 'counting to ten' tactic.

The British relaxation expert Jane Madders recommends that when you're really getting worked up:

1. Say 'stop' to yourself.
2. Breathe in deeply and breathe out slowly. As you do so, drop your shoulders and relax your hands.
3. Breathe in deeply again and, as you breathe out, make sure your teeth aren't clenched tightly together.
4. Take two small quiet breaths.[45]

Take breaks. Even if you have a looming deadline, it's advisable to give yourself breathing space – it doesn't have to be for long. Stare out of the window, talk to someone you like, anything.

Diet and exercise

Yes, I know, you can't open any magazine or paper these days without being told off about your diet – less sugar, fat and salt and more fibre and all that – and not doing enough exercise. However, the evidence is that physical fitness really does offer some protection against the damaging effects of stress.[46] One study with American undergraduates, for example, found that among those who'd had a very stressful year, the physically fit felt less depressed and had fewer health problems than did those who were less fit.[47]

Dr Hugh Bethell, a British coronary rehabilitation expert, advises on the way to get fit:

> You must find a game or a sport which you enjoy. If necessary, try several. Those which bring most benefit are the dynamic (aerobic) ones like running, swimming, cycling, circuit training, dancing, football, hockey. But beware those like squash which involve bursts of intense effort. Start at a low level and build up gradually. You

should aim to do your chosen activity three or four times weekly, for at least 20 to 30 minutes, sufficiently vigorously to keep you short of breath.[48]

But *don't* overdo it. Before you start on any unaccustomed exercise, its always best to consult your doctor.

When you've been working hard and you need a fast reviver, rather than reaching for that chocolate biscuit 'just to keep you going', take a short brisk walk instead. The evidence is that it will restore your energy much better. Psychologist Robert Thayer of California State University at Long Beach got student volunteers either to eat a candy bar or to walk rapidly for ten minutes on twelve selected days.[49] They were asked to rate their energy, tiredness and tension just before snacking or walking and then at intervals during the following two hours.

Thayer found that the sugar snack increased energy and reduced tiredness for the first half hour; but after that, energy dropped off and tiredness increased. What's more, eating the candy bar resulted in *higher* tension for two hours afterwards. Following the brisk walk, on the other hand, the volunteers reported raised energy and *decreased* tiredness and tension for two hours.

So sling the sweetmeats and pound the pavements when you feel it all getting to you . . .

Don't let work take over

One of the dangerous tendencies of stressful work is that it can crawl, amoeba-like, all over your private life. It might seem crashingly obvious to say 'don't let it'. But people *do* develop bad habits like always taking work home with them, never being seen without a bulging briefcase, thinking about work all the time. Not only will this almost certainly be driving any nearest and dearest you may have completely round the bend – not good for a stress-free home life – but it can affect you directly, too.

Research shows that being able rapidly to let go of your stress and tension at the end of the working day results in fewer signs of ill-health. Robert Baron says:

> Fortunately, there are several concrete steps people can take to help master this skill. For example, they can make it a rule to leave work at the office rather than bringing it home with them. Similarly, they can cultivate hobbies and other leisure-time activities that will distract them from re-living the day once it is over. Through these and related steps, individuals can help assure that they will have at least *some* time away from the cares and woes of their jobs – a period during which they can rest and recuperate. The advantages of establishing such 'islands of tranquility' in a busy life are too obvious to require further comment.[50]

Quite.

Negotiate home responsibilities

Sadly, unless you have a staff of thousands plus butler, there is work to be done at home too. Shopping, cooking, cleaning, childcare, etc., etc., etc. It is, disgracefully, still the case that in dual-career couples, the woman usually does more than her fair share of the 'home work', and suffers extra stress as a consequence. (I'll have more to say about this in the next chapter.) It's *vital*, if you have a partner and perhaps children too, to negotiate a fair way of dividing or rotating your duties at home. Do anything you can not only to make sure that home duties are fairly distributed but to organize time for fun and relaxation – really the best recipes for a less-stressed life.

Domestic tasks can be a problem if you live alone, too. One of Cary Cooper and Marilyn Davidson's interviewees, a forty-three-year-old top executive and single woman, told them:

> Although I enjoy living alone, I have to do a lot of socializing and working in the evenings, and not having a

'wife' at home is one of the most stressful things for me and the other single working women I know. Unlike my male colleagues who are all married, I have no one to help with my shopping, cleaning and entertaining. The way I cope with this is to plan my time very carefully.

Cooper and Davidson comment: 'It seems that women in this situation appear to cope best when they organise and allocate times in their working week to specific domestic, social and relaxation periods – and stick to them!'[51]

Time management

One of the most stressful things in our working lives is that dreadful, oppressive sensation that you're not on top of things, that there's never enough time to get everything done, that you can only survive by working twelve hours a day. For example, one constant stressor can be that mouldering, unpleasant-looking pile of paper that seems to breed overnight and flutter at you accusingly all day. A way of dealing with this is to learn the skills of 'time management'.

The American time management experts Helen Reynolds and Mary Tramel have lots of ideas on how to keep your paperwork from accumulating. Perhaps the most important is *'Never handle a piece of paper more than once*. Every time you pick up a piece of paper, whether it is a letter, a report, a phone message, do something with it other than putting it in a "to do" pile. If it is a letter that requires your reply, answer it *now*. If it is a report that you need to read and digest, do it *now*.'[52] If you don't have time to read it now, they suggest, delegate it to someone else who can summarize it for you.

However, we are not all lucky enough to have an assistant to do these sorts of things for us. What might help is to set aside a fixed period each day to deal with paperwork. Do it then and only then; but *every day*. That way, you can keep the wretched stuff from piling up to depressing, unmanageable heights. It's also worth remembering that a quick phone call may be faster than a letter; and confining what you have to say to a business postcard or compliment slip will stop you spreading yourself unnecessarily over a large sheet of writing paper.

According to John Adair, a British expert on leadership skills, what could be very salutary is to keep a precise time diary for a while of what exactly you do in your working day. You may then realize that you're spending too long on phone calls, chatting to colleagues and to people dropping in, slowly reading (as opposed to scanning) routine reports, and so on. Then you can cut down on time-wasting and work out priorities.

Adair has some other pertinent points too. Though directed at managers, they are valid whatever your place in the hierarchy:

Make the most of your best time
Programme important tasks for the time of day you function best. Have planned quiet periods for creative thinking.

Capitalise on marginal time
Squeeze activities into the minutes you spend waiting for a train or between meetings.

Avoid clutter
Try re-organising your desk for effectiveness. Sort papers into categories according to action priorities. Generate as little paper as possible yourself.

Do it now
'Procrastination is the thief of time'
'My object was always to do the business of the day in the day' (Wellington)

Learn to say No
Do not let others misappropriate your time.
Decline tactfully but firmly to avoid over-commitment.

Delegate
Learn to delegate as much as possible.[53]

Perhaps the most important advice boils down to 'Don't be too much of a perfectionist'. In the book based on a Channel 4 television series presented by Professor Cary Cooper, *How to Survive the 9–5*, the authors put it like this:

> The secret of stress management, as any successful news journalist will tell you, is to *pace* yourself. Set yourself your own clear, personal, realistic objectives, and avoid conflicting goals. Don't work at eleven-tenths of your capacity, if you really have to push – work at nine-tenths. Keep some energy in reserve. Take breaks – never work till you drop. Plan ahead as much as you can, order your priorities and don't be afraid to make lists. If in doubt about what to do decide *now* and act on your decision immediately – you might sometimes be wrong but that's not the end of the world – use the experience and press on, but never look back and reproach yourself. Be flexible, and don't be too hard on yourself if you can only do the job to second-class standards under difficult conditions. That will almost certainly do fine.[54]

'Type A' personalities

And what of the famous 'type A' coronary-prone personality? Type As are usually defined as competitive, hard-driving, aggressive strivers who constantly feel under pressure of time, and who are more vulnerable to coronary heart disease – a known stress-related illness – than are the more laid-back Type Bs.[55]

Type As, for example, incline to:

1. Speaking with impatience
2. Hurried walking and eating
3. A chronic sense of time urgency
4. Feeling guilty when relaxing
5. Being focused on one's own interests to the exclusion of other people and the surroundings

Type Bs, in contrast, are those who:

1. Do not suffer from a sense of urgency
2. Do not harbor hostility
3. Can play for fun and relaxation rather than competition
4. Can relax without guilt[56]

General prescriptions for dealing with Type A traits always sound extremely reasonable but are not always easy to follow. In addition to stress management techniques that are recommended for everyone, such as relaxation, breaks, time management, exercise and *having fun*, Cary Cooper suggests the following to Type As:

Do only one thing at a time. Don't try to work and eat, for example.

Do not feel you always have to be right.

Give more thought to the needs of others.

Try to restrain yourself from constantly talking. Really listen to others and don't try to finish their sentences.

Don't expect perfection in yourself or others. It will only make you frustrated and hostile.

Use traffic jams and other potentially irritating situations to take some deep breaths and relax.[57]

The last two prescriptions may be particularly important. Evidence is mounting that the really critical strand of the Type A personality which endangers health is, in fact, hostility. Hostility may emerge as, say, being rude, argumentative, condescending, making harsh generalizations, and in angry responses to common frustrations like waiting in queues or being caught behind a slow moving car.[58] Type As become angry and irritable too easily, and – particularly if they usually try to hide it – this increases their chances of a heart attack.[59]

According to Professor Cooper, 'The World Health Organization has published figures which indicate that not only is the United Kingdom near the top of the world league table in terms of mortality due to heart disease, but also is showing substantial yearly increases.'[60]

Ouch. Time for us all to get a grip.

Getting it all in perspective

D'you think I did well in there? Gosh, thanks. It was nothing. I mean, I'd been preparing that speech for weeks. I'd wake up with a start in the night and find myself mouthing paragraph 2.

It's all gone wrong. The boss muttered something about that report 'not being one of my best efforts'. I knew he wouldn't like it. The minute I sat down to type 'Introduction: the background', I was overcome by this awful sense of doom.

How's it going? Oh, excellently, thanks. I'm being put up for promotion a year early. Other bits of my life aren't going so well, though, I have to say. My other half is rather peeved with me, and keeps going on about 'my priorities' and why the hell had I to go to a business meeting in Holland on our anniversary last week. I'm starting to feel torn in two.

Success, failure, achievement – how much do they matter? One of your motives in reading this book may have been that you wanted to know how to 'get on' – I hope it will have helped you with that. But I did have something much more significant in mind. I wanted to show how it's possible to get more enjoyment and satisfaction out of your working life – and 'doing well' is only one aspect.

It is, however, for many of us, quite an important aspect. In this last chapter I want to focus specifically on the way we think about our successes and failures, and the implications for our future achievements. Finally, I examine that most difficult topic, the blending and balance of our work and personal lives.

SUCCESS AND FAILURE

When we succeed or fail at something we do, we tend to attribute our successes to 'internal' factors such as our ability or the effort we put into it, and our failures to 'external' factors like 'frightfully bad luck', the impossibility of the task, the boss's unreasonably high standards, the fact that an earthquake destroyed our filing cabinet containing all the vital papers, and so on.

Of course, as the social psychologist Leonard Berkowitz says, 'For most of us there are limits to the degree that we engage in this kind of wishful thinking. We don't "kid ourselves" completely and don't claim credit for every one of our successes or deny responsibility for each failure. The self-serving bias is most likely to operate when it is unclear just what led to the particular outcome.'[1]

But such situations are hardly uncommon. Bernard Weiner, an American psychologist who has done a lot of work on the attributions we make for success and failure, has a lovely example of this 'self-serving bias' in operation. He quotes from the *Los Angeles Times*:

> Here it is Thanksgiving week, and the Los Angeles Rams are looking like the biggest turkeys in town. Coach Ray Malavasi has eliminated bad luck, biorhythms, and sunspots as the reasons why his football team has lost 9 of its last 10 games. Now he's considering the unthinkable possibilities that: (a) he has lousy players or (b) they aren't really trying.[2]

The self-serving bias is a very useful little tendency: it allows us to protect or boost our self-esteem and our public image.[3]

However, some people seem not to cosset their egos that way, and this can have sad psychological consequences. Those who – for whatever reason – don't think very highly of themselves, maintain their low self-esteem by doing exactly the opposite of the self-serving bias. In other words, they tend to put their successes down to external factors and their failures down to internal ones.[4] 'Yes, I know the boss was pleased with my presentation. But it was such an easy topic, the effects of destruction of the rain forests on atmospheric oxygen levels – honestly, anyone could have done it.' Or: 'God, it was *catastrophic*. I'd put up this idea about reprogramming the computer to do the estimates a different way, and the accounts department didn't like it at all. I'm so stupid, I think it'd be best for everyone if I just stapled my lips together.'

It's also possible, as 'Type A' personalities tend to do (see p. 161), to set unrealistically high standards or goals for yourself.[5] So you might, on top of any other unfortunate tendencies, count as a failure what others might have been perfectly happy with.

The precise attributions we make for our past successes and failures affect not just our self-esteem but also our future expectations. Clearly, our beliefs about our past performance on a specific task will affect how well we think we're going to do on a similar (or related) task in the future. In particular, how 'stable' (i.e., unlikely to change) we think the cause of that past performance was. If we attribute success to a stable cause, or failure to an unstable cause, then we're more likely to expect success in the future than if we put our failure down to a stable cause, or success to an unstable cause.[6]

So, for instance, we'd expect success again if we put our triumph down to a stable cause like aptitude. 'Ya, the MD *really* liked my suggestion for boosting sales by giving away free pedicure vouchers with every packet of diamante-tiger encrusted tights. But then, I've always been an ideas person, and the sparkly socks campaign should be no problem.'

If we've failed and put it down to our innate lack of ability or the unalterable difficulty of the task, then that's not going to change, so why bother to try? 'When I fed in my new

computer program, all our invoices started printing out in
Gothic script. I think my brain cells must have gone into
early retirement. I'm really going to have to give up all this
high-tech stuff before I make a terminal blunder.'

But if you put your past performance down to an unstable
cause – such as (in the case of failure) low effort, bad mood,
fatigue or appalling luck – then that has no implications for
the future. 'Hell, if I'd put a bit more effort into it, it would
have been fine. Starting to work on that briefing at eight
o'clock the previous night after sneaking out all day to watch
the cricket at Lord's was perhaps not too good a strategy. I'll
remember not to do *that* again.'

Research shows not only that the attributions we make
really do affect our performance, but also that self-destructive
attributions can be changed for the better.[7] When people who
typically put failure down to their own inadequacies (i.e.,
lasting, internal causes) are encouraged to start attributing it
to external or temporary factors, then they're more likely to
stop regarding failure as inevitable. (It's generally better to
believe, say, that you have failed because you didn't try hard
enough than that you're just incapable of doing it.) As a
result, they become more persistent in their efforts to succeed
– and their performance improves.

The problem with a pessimistic outlook is that it traps you
in a negative, self-fulfilling circle. 'I'm no good, that's why I
failed, so I'm *bound* to fail again. I'm not going to bother to
put much effort into it, there's no point. Oh gosh, what do
you know, I *have* failed again. I knew it. I think I'll just retire
to the country and grow mangel-wurzels. Mind you, I'd
probably make a pig's ear of that, too.'

The first step towards breaking out of a self-destructive
psychological trap is to recognize that you're in it in the first
place. But once you've done that you will find – with practice
– that you can learn to stop thinking in this debilitating,
helplessness-inducing way.

WORK v. PERSONAL LIFE

Success and achievement are only part of the working experience, and work is only part of life. But balancing the demands of work and our personal lives can be the most difficult task of all.

I was talking the other day to a man – let's call him Chris – whose boss is a workaholic. He works from about 8 a.m. to 8.30 or 9 p.m. every day, and takes work home at the weekends. Chris was trying hard to convince me that his boss was a happy man. 'He enjoys his work. What's wrong with doing it all the time? Who's to say that's not the best life for him?'

Theoretically, no one. But I found it hard to believe. Close questioning ensued. Under interrogation, Chris revealed the constantly replenished store of indigestion tablets which the boss kept in his desk drawer; and the not-irrelevant fact that he had a wife. A *wife*? Really? What did she do, carry a photograph of him around with her so she'd be sure to recognize him if she bumped into him in the bathroom? Oh – and he had two children too? Is your boss quite sure about that? I mean, one or two extra haven't arrived when he wasn't looking?

Living alone

Even if Chris's boss had been on his own, a life devoted to work, sleep and indigestion tablets hardly seems a top-quality existence. This is an extreme example, of course, but such a lifestyle can be easy to slip into. According to the unattached women managers whom Cary Cooper and Marilyn Davidson interviewed for their study (see p. 158–9), 'it is all too easy to fall into the habit of spending late evenings at the office and taking more and more work home, when living alone'.

These women coped best when they allocated themselves specific periods in the week for fun, relaxation and domestic duties – and stuck to them resolutely. They were determined not to let their work take over, and made positive use of the space they made for themselves.

> For many unattached women managers, living alone gave them freedom and 'room to grow'. However, for others, the isolation they experienced was sometimes intense, and they emphasized the importance of cultivating a network of supportive friends: 'The most stressful part about being a single career woman is the isolation, somebody to talk to when you get home about your work. The loneliness of not having this is sometimes intense and is for me the major stress factor in my life. The only way I have found to cope with this is by having a large network of friends, some of them are in the same situation as me.[8]

These points obviously don't apply just to women or to managers. If you live alone, your non-work time can be used to greatly enhance your life by developing your own interests and pleasures and making and maintaining friendships. Friends are a source of great satisfaction, fun and support; and research shows they are good for our psychological *and* physical health.[9]

Living with a partner

Matters become more complicated, to say the least, if you live with someone. Especially if that partner works too – an increasingly common pattern.

Research on dual-earner couples shows that, as you'd expect, managing your lives together can be a real struggle. It also reveals that women, even today, tend to draw the short straw. The evidence is that women in full-time employment still retain major domestic responsibilities, whether they're parents or not.[10] 'Yes, darling, I did clinch the deal, the lemon chicken's in the oven, the children are washed and I've wiped up Sam's sick, *don't* put your muddy feet on the kitchen floor, I've just mopped it . . .'

Statistics published by the Central Statistical Office illustrate the point. In Great Britain in 1985, full-time employees used their time in a typical week as follows:

Weekly hours spent on:	Males	Females
Employment and travel to and from place of work	45.0	40.8
Essential activities	33.1	45.1
Sleep	56.4	57.5
Free time	33.5	24.6

'Essential activities' were defined as: 'Essential domestic work and personal care. This includes cooking, essential shopping, child care, eating meals, washing, and getting up and going to bed.'[11]

What effect can this imbalance have?

A major, long-term investigation of heart disease is being done at Framingham, Massachusetts, whose inhabitants have been undergoing regular medical screening since the 1950s.[12] Results have revealed that working women did not suffer from coronary heart disease more than housewives, and their rates were lower than for working men. But when the researchers compared married working women with children against those without children it emerged that the incidence of heart disease rose as the number of children increased. This was not the case for housewives. The pressure of work *plus* home *plus children* can increase stress to dangerous levels.

But there can be problems whether children are present or not. The research further showed that working women as a whole 'experienced more daily stress, marital dissatisfaction, and aging worries and were less likely to show overt anger than either housewives or men'.[13] Other studies, too, have found that 'marital adjustment' is worse for dual-career wives than for non-employed wives.[14]

This is clearly not good enough. Where is the New Man? The one who happily does his fair share of the domestic chores and childcare? Not arrived, apparently.[15]

The image of designer parenthood these days is of the father joyfully changing nappies, taking the toddler to nursery and the eight-year-old to tap-dancing classes, helping little Johnny with his Lego, piling Susie into her clothes and frying the morning eggs and bacon for his merry brood.

Nice thought; and it's true that fathers *are* doing more with their children than they used to. It has become expected that they do; and, of course, more and more women with children are going out to work.

But what are the effects of fathers' greater participation? Are they basking in a warm glow of self-fulfilment? Are wives relieved that they no longer have the stresses of running a job and the home single-handed? Even if they do not go out to work, isn't it wonderful to have their husbands joining in and lightening the burdens of full-time motherhood?

Well, no, seems to be the answer. It's more likely that she feels guilty and he feels resentful. This is the depressing implication of an American study done by psychologists Grace Baruch and Rosalind Barnett.[16] They interviewed 160 middle-class married couples, all of whom had at least one young child; most had two or three.

The researchers looked at eleven childcare tasks: 'taking to birthday party, taking to doctor/dentist, going to teacher conference, supervising morning routine, cleaning up room, spending special time at bedtime, taking to or from lessons, buying clothes, taking on outing (museum, park), supervising personal hygiene, and staying home or making arrangements for care when child is sick'.

What they found was that the more fathers took part in these activities, the more they felt that their wives were failing in their duties as mothers and that childcare was interfering with their own work.

In the so-called liberated 1980s, this is really terrific news. The men managed to feel resentful despite the fact that their wives still did far more for their children than they did, whether the women worked or not. Half the women in the sample were full-time mothers, and half were employed outside the home. Of the latter, thirty-seven worked thirty or more hours per week; nearly all the rest worked between seventeen and a half and twenty-nine hours a week.

The women were well aware of their husbands' feelings; the more a man helped to look after his offspring, the more his wife saw him as being dissatisfied with her allocation of time to the children. And 'helped' is the operative word here; the men rarely took responsibility for the children in terms of 'remembering, planning and scheduling' the various childcare tasks.

Fathers spending time alone with their young ones seemed to have particularly bad effects. Not only did it make them more critical of their wives as parents, but it also made their wives feel less satisfied with their lives as a whole.

The full-time mothers felt guilty if they did not carry the whole burden of children, and the employed women, in the grip of the ghastly 'superwoman' notion – that you should be able to run a job with one hand, the children with the other and the house with whatever part of the anatomy is left – felt inadequate for not being able to do it.

One of the study's other findings, on 'housecare' rather than childcare, reinforces the point. The men didn't do much of what the researchers call 'traditionally feminine chores': 'meal preparation, cleaning house, laundry, grocery shopping and meal cleanup'. But the more they did it, the more their wives, if employed, reported 'that their own work interfered with their family responsibilities'.

So the wives were feeling guilty about their husbands

sharing the domestic work as well as the care of their children. But weren't the fathers getting satisfaction out of spending time with their offspring, regardless of whether or not their wives were present?

Apparently not. The study showed that the more a father spent time with his children, the more involved and competent he felt as a parent. But this did not increase his satisfaction with *being* a parent. 'Daily involvement with a child,' Grace Baruch and Rosalind Barnett say, 'may force a man to face the problems as well as the pleasures of the parental role, problems well known to women.'[17]

If this rather alarming snapshot of dual-earner family life is generally applicable, then it's no wonder that the lifestyle itself is being blamed as the main culprit of the dramatically rising divorce rates.[18]

But it really doesn't have to be like this. For both partners to work and share their domestic responsibilities equally isn't an impossible dream, for heaven's sake. But it certainly requires some radical changes in attitude . . .

It'll be hardest if you have young children. But normally you will have both agreed to have them, and no one expects child-rearing to be one long party. What is important is to be open with each other in uncovering hidden guilt and resentment, and to *negotiate* the best way to conduct your lives together.

In *How to Survive the 9–5*, the authors provide some sound general suggestions on coping with a dual career relationship:

1. Discuss what you'd like from your work and home lives. Understand the effects your needs have on your partner's freedom of action.

2. Try to limit your needs so both have some degree of freedom and an opportunity to cope.

3. Make long-term plans to keep work/home conflicts to a minimum.

4. Compartmentalise your work and home lives – again reducing conflicts.

5. Make flexible career plans around yourself rather than any organisation – be prepared to move, change, retrain.[19]

Part of the secret of coping, of course, is simply organising the everyday practicalities. On the basis of their study of women managers, Cary Cooper and Marilyn Davidson say:

> In dual career couples, careful planning and organization can help to alleviate some of the domestic pressures. A particular couple, for example, spent on average only one morning a week on cooking and shopping between them. They employed someone to clean the house twice a week, and each Saturday morning one of them would cook the following week's meals and store them in the freezer, while the other did the week's shopping. Consequently, besides heating up the meal, evenings after work were free for leisure and relaxation.[20]

Of course, many people don't earn enough money to pay for help or even a freezer. But the principle of open discussion and negotiation still applies – and it applies whether or not you have children. It may be that what needs to be resolved is not just how you share and divide domestic tasks but whether one or both of you is spending more time on work than is good for either of you.

You could, if you liked, conduct the discussion semi-formally. Professor Cary Cooper suggests a possible strategy:

Step 1. Prepare balance sheet of work and home commitments (listing details of hours spent, tasks undertaken, etc.).

Step 2. Call formal family meeting to share concerns and detailed balance sheet.

Step 3. Re-negotiate various family commitments.

Step 4. Create mutual action plans for the next three months, which are agreed by all family members.

Step 5. Review success or otherwise of action plans at the end of three-month period.

Step 6. Develop new action plans based on experience of previous one. Continue process until all parties are more or less satisfied with arrangements.[21]

And it seems to me vital, in the course of your negotiations, to build in time for pleasure, fun, friends and interests. Sleep, work and domestic drudgery isn't exactly a high-quality mixture. Building in some time to *talk* to each other – about work problems, gossip, whatever – isn't a bad idea either . . .

For women, the currently overburdened ones, the benefits of sharing responsibilities are obvious. For men, though it might mean more domestic work and childcare, it could also bring a more rounded, involved and happy lifestyle, with a less stressed and perhaps happier marriage, and the chance to develop – through sharing the messy and difficult as well as the delightful bits of child-rearing – as a responsible human being.

And women must not feel guilty when men do what is, after all, only their fair share. You have just as much right to a satisfying and successful career as your partner; and, more than likely, you both need the money, too. As for male resentment, probably the best way to deal with it is to drag it out into the open. It should eventually wither away under the harsh light of scrutiny.

There is no way that family life is ever going to revert to the 'traditional' pattern. With time, perhaps men and women will stop expecting things of themselves and each other that are unrealistic, and start taking *joint* responsibility for their lives together.

A sense of perspective

Developing a sense of perspective on the role work plays in your life can be hard to do. Of course it matters – you must think so, or you wouldn't be reading this book in the first place. And work can provide much pleasure and gratification as well as struggle and stress. But other parts of life can provide great benefits too – why squeeze them out? And if you're having a problem at work, by stepping back and seeing it in the broad context of your long and multi-faceted life you will diminish its importance. 'Yeah, I did have a row with the boss today. But I'm going to what promises to be a great party tomorrow, my son's just won his school medal for the best essay on "What's Wrong with My Parents", I adore my husband, my backhand's improving – and anyway the whole silly thing'll have blown over by next week.'

There's evidence that having a many-sided view of yourself can be very good for you when you're under stress. If you can see yourself in lots of distinct ways – as worker, lover, friend, parent, tennis player, gardener, and so on – you will be less likely to feel depressed, stressed and ill after experiencing a high level of stressful events than you will if you limit your self-image to only one or two roles, such as worker and spouse.[22]

Developing a rounded life will, in any case, be much more satisfying. If work ever threatens to overwhelm you, tell yourself that it'll all be the same in thirty years. The point is, are you having a good time now?

NOTES AND REFERENCES

1 Into the maelstrom

1. Charles Lamb, letter to Barton, September 1822.
2. Heller, J., *Something Happened* (London: Corgi, 1974), pp. 36, 72.
3. Warr, P., 'A national study of non-financial employment commitment', *Journal of Occupational Psychology*, 55 (1982), pp. 297–312.
4. Wodehouse, P. G., *Psmith in the City* (Harmondsworth, Middlesex: Penguin, 1970), p. 65. First published by A. & C. Black, 1910.
5. Quoted in Metcalf, F., *The Penguin Dictionary of Modern Humorous Quotations* (London: Penguin, 1986).
6. For more of the same see Hewison, W. (ed.), *Funny Business: Punch in the Office* (London: Grafton, 1986).

2 Colleagues – how to get on with them

1. Baron, R. A. and Byrne, D., *Social Psychology* (5th edn., Boston: Allyn and Bacon, 1987), p. 197.
2. Landy, D. and Sigall, H., 'Beauty is talent: task evaluation as a function of the performer's physical attractiveness', *Journal of Personality and Social Psychology*, 29 (1974), pp. 299–304.
3. Snyder, M. L., Tanke, E. D. and Berscheid, E., 'Social perception and interpersonal behavior: on the self-fulfilling nature of social stereotypes', *Journal of Personality and Social Psychology*, 35 (1977), pp. 656–66.
4. Abbott, A. R. and Sebastian, R. J., 'Physical attractiveness and expectations of success', *Personality and Social Psychology Bulletin*, 7 (1981), pp. 481–6.
5. Goldman, W. and Lewis, P., 'Beautiful is good: evidence that the physically attractive are more socially skillful', *Journal of Experimental Social Psychology*, 13 (1977), pp. 125–30.
6. Reis, H. T., Nezlek, J. and Wheeler, L., 'Physical attractiveness in social interaction', *Journal of Personality and Social Psychology*, 38 (1980), pp. 604–17; Reis, H. T., Wheeler, L., Spiegel, N., Kernis, M. H., Nezlek, J. and Perri, M., 'Physical attractiveness in social interaction: I. Why does appearance affect social experience?', *Journal of Personality and Social*

Psychology, **43** (1982), pp. 979–96.

7. Webster, M. and Driskell, J. E., 'Beauty as status', *American Journal of Sociology*, **89** (1983), pp. 140–65.

8. See e.g. Harris, M. B., Harris, R. J. and Bochner, S., 'Fat, four-eyed, and female: stereotypes of obesity, glasses, and gender', *Journal of Applied Social Psychology*, **12** (1982), pp. 503–16.

9. Mueser, K. T., Grau, B. W., Sussman, S. and Rosen, A. J., 'You're only as pretty as you feel: facial expression as a determinant of physical attractiveness', *Journal of Personality and Social Psychology*, **46** (1984), pp. 469–78.

10. See e.g. Timmerman, K. and Hewitt, J., 'Examining the halo effect of physical attractiveness', *Perceptual and Motor Skills*, **51** (1980), pp. 607–12.

11. See Graham, J. A. and Kligman, A. M. (eds.), *The Psychology of Cosmetic Treatments* (New York: Praeger, 1985).

12. Nisbett, R. E. and Wilson, T. D., 'The halo effect: evidence for unconscious alteration of judgments', *Journal of Personality and Social Psychology*, **35** (1977), pp. 250–6.

13. Webster, M. and Driskell, J. E., 'Beauty as status', p. 159.

14. Forsythe, S., Drake, M. F. and Cox, C. E., 'Influence of applicant's dress on interviewer's selection decisions', *Journal of Applied Psychology*, **70** (1985), pp. 374–8.

15. Dion, K., Berscheid, E. and Walster, E., 'What is beautiful is good', *Journal of Personality and Social Psychology*, **24** (1972), pp. 285–90.

16. Heilman, M. E. and Saruwatari, L. R., 'When beauty is beastly: the effects of appearance and sex on evaluations of job applicants for managerial and nonmanagerial jobs', *Organizational Behavior and Human Performance*, **23** (1979), pp. 360–72.

17. See e.g. Cash, T. F. and Kilcullen, R. N., 'The aye of the beholder: susceptibility to sexism and beautyism in the evaluation of managerial applicants', *Journal of Applied Social Psychology*, **15** (1985), pp. 591–605.

18. Heilman, M. E. and Saruwatari, L. R., 'When beauty is beastly'.

19. Webster, M. and Driskell, J. E., 'Beauty as status'.

20. Gillen, B., 'Physical attractiveness: a determinant of two types of goodness', *Personality and Social Psychology Bulletin*, **7** (1981), pp. 277–81.

21. McElroy, J. C., Morrow, P.

C. and Wall., L. C., 'Generalizing impact of object language to other audiences: peer response to office design', *Psychological Reports*, 53 (1983), pp. 315–22.

22. *Ibid.*

23. Campbell, D. E., 'Interior office design and visitor response', *Journal of Applied Psychology*, 64 (1979), pp. 648–53.

24. See Sundstrom, E., *Work Places* (Cambridge University Press, 1986), pp. 303–7.

25. Goodrich, R., 'Seven office evaluations: a review', *Environment and Behavior*, 14 (1982), pp. 364, 367.

26. For a review see e.g. Baron, R. A. and Byrne, D., *Social Psychology*, pp. 436–40.

27. Hall, E. T., *The Hidden Dimension* (New York: Doubleday, 1966).

28. Hall, E. T., *The Silent Language* (New York: Doubleday, 1959).

29. Stewart, R., *Managers and Their Jobs* (London: Macmillan, 1967).

30. Argyle, M., and Henderson, M., *The Anatomy of Relationships* (Harmondsworth, Middlesex: Penguin, 1985), p. 244.

31. Argyle, M. *The Social Psychology of Work* (Harmondsworth, Middlesex: Penguin, 1972).

32. Repetti, R. L., 'Individual and common components of the social environment at work and psychological well-being', *Journal of Personality and Social Psychology*, 52 (1987), pp. 710–20.

33. Adapted from Argyle, M. and Henderson, M., 'The rules of relationships', chapter in Duck, S. and Perlman, D. (eds.), *Understanding Personal Relationships* (London: Sage, 1985), table 1 on p. 71.

34. For more on social skills see e.g. Argyle, M., *The Psychology of Interpersonal Behaviour* (4th edn., Harmondsworth, Middlesex: Penguin, 1983); Duck, S., *Human Relationships* (London: Sage, 1983).

35. Adapted from Argyle, M. and Henderson, M., *The Anatomy of Relationships*, p. 255.

36. Henderson, M. and Argyle, M., 'Social support by four categories of work colleagues: relationships between activities, stress and satisfaction', *Journal of Occupational Behaviour*, 6 (1985), pp. 230–1.

37. Source: Argyle, M. and Henderson, M., *The Anatomy of Relationships*, p. 265.

38. See e.g. Berkowitz, L., *A Survey of Social Psychology* (3rd edn., New York: Holt, Rinehart and Winston, 1986), pp. 86–91.

39. For more on the self-fulfilling

prophecy see e.g. Lloyd, P.,
Mayes, A., Manstead, A. S.
R., Meudell, P. R. and
Wagner, H. L., *Introduction
to Psychology* (London:
Fontana, 1984), pp. 604,
640–2.

40. Baron, R. A. and Byrne, D.,
Social Psychology, p. 57. For
more on attribution processes
see e.g. Berkowitz, L., *A
Survey of Social Psychology*,
pp. 154–62.

41. See e.g. Baron, R. A. and
Byrne, D., *Social Psychology*,
pp. 493–8.

42. Turner, J. C., 'Social
identification and
psychological group
formation', chapter in Tajfel,
H. (ed.), *The Social
Dimension*, vol. 2
(Cambridge University Press,
1984), p. 529.

43. See e.g. Deaux, K. and
Wrightsman, L. S., *Social
Psychology in the 80s* (4th
edn., Monterey, California:
Brooks/Cole, 1984), p. 149.

44. US Merit Systems Protection
Board, *Sexual Harassment in
the Federal Workplace: is it a
problem?* (Washington, D.C.:
Superintendent of
Documents, US Government
Printing Office, 1981).

45. See Cooper, C. L. and
Davidson, M. J., *High
Pressure* (London: Fontana,
1982), pp. 100–1.

46. See Read, S., *Sexual
Harassment at Work*
(Feltham, Middlesex:
Hamlyn, 1982), pp. 144–5.

47. Gutek, B. A. and Morasch,
B., 'Sex-ratios, sex-role
spillover, and sexual
harassment of women at
work', *Journal of Social
Issues*, 38 (1982), pp. 55–74.

48. Tangri, S. S., Burt, M. R. and
Johnson, L. B., 'Sexual
harassment at work: three
explanatory models', *Journal
of Social Issues*, 38 (1982),
pp. 33–54.

49. Abbey, A., 'Sex differences in
attributions for friendly
behavior: do males
misperceive females'
friendliness?', *Journal of
Personality and Social
Psychology*, 42 (1982),
pp. 830–8.

50. See e.g. *Sex in the Office: an
investigation into the
incidence of sexual
harassment* (London:
Statistical Services Division,
Alfred Marks Bureau, 1982);
Read, S., *Sexual Harassment
at Work*; Renick, J. C.,
'Sexual harassment at work:
why it happens, what to do
about it', *Personnel Journal*,
59 (1980), pp. 658–62.

51. Surveys done in 1982 by the
Camden and Liverpool
branches of the National and
Local Government Officers
Association; Tangri, S. S. et
al., 'Sexual harassment at
work'.

52. See e.g. US Merit Systems
Protection Board, *Sexual
Harassment in the Federal
Workplace*.

53. See e.g. 'Sexual harassment: you tell us, it's *not* a joke', *Cosmopolitan*, October 1982, pp. 153, 155; Renick, J. C., 'Sexual harassment at work'.

54. For more on sexual harassment see Tysoe, M., 'The sexual harassers', *New Society*, 4 November 1982, pp. 212–13.

55. Harrison, R. and Lee, R., 'Love at work', *Personnel Management* (1986), pp. 20–4.

56. See e.g. Baron, R. A. and Byrne, D., *Social Psychology*, pp. 188–92.

57. Quinn, R. E., 'Coping with Cupid: the formation, impact, and management of romantic relationships in organizations', *Administrative Science Quarterly*, **22** (1977), pp. 30–45.

3 Subordinates – how to motivate them

1. For reviews of psychological research on leadership see e.g. Baron, R. A., *Behavior in Organizations* (2nd edn., Boston: Allyn and Bacon, 1986), chapter 9; Bryman, A., *Leadership and Organizations* (London: Routledge and Kegan Paul, 1986); Yetton, P., 'Leadership and supervision', chapter in Gruneberg, M. and Wall, T., *Social Psychology and Organisational Behaviour* (Chichester: John Wiley, 1984).

2. Baron R. A., *Behavior in Organizations*, p. 288.

3. For a review see Bryman, A., *Leadership and Organizations*.

4. Adapted from Scandura, T. A. and Graen, G. B., 'Moderating effects of initial leader–member exchange status on the effects of a leadership intervention', *Journal of Applied Psychology*, **69** (1984), pp. 428–36.

5. Baron, R. A., *Behavior in Organizations*, p. 326.

6. Scandura, T. A. and Graen, G. B., 'Moderating effects of initial leader–member exchange status on the effects of a leadership intervention'.

7. Baron, R. A., *Behavior in Organizations*, p. 288.

8. See e.g. Bryman, A., *Leadership and Organizations*.

9. See Bryman, A., *Leadership and Organizations*.

10. See Field, R. H. G., 'A test of the Vroom–Yetton normative model of leadership', *Journal of Applied Psychology*, **67** (1982), pp. 523–32; Vroom, V. H. and Jago, A. G., 'On the validity of the Vroom–Yetton model', *Journal of Applied Psychology*, **63** (1978), pp. 151–62.

11. Yetton, P., 'Leadership and supervision', p. 26.

12. Adapted from Vroom, V. H. and Jago, A. G., 'On the validity of the Vroom–Yetton model', p. 152.

13. *Ibid.*, Vroom, V. H. and Jago, A. G., 'On the validity of the Vroom–Yetton model', p. 153 (with sexist wording eliminated).

14. Baron, R. A., *Behavior in Organizations*, p. 288; see also Heilman, M. E., Hornstein, H. A., Cage, J. H. and Herschlag, J. K., 'Reactions to prescribed leader behavior as a function of role perspective: the case of the Vroom–Yetton model', *Journal of Applied Psychology*, **69** (1984), pp. 50–60.

15. Mento, A. J., Steel, R. P. and Karren, R. J., 'A meta-analytic study of the effects of goal setting on task performance: 1966–1984', *Organizational Behavior and Human Decision Processes*, **39** (1987), pp. 52–83; Tubbs, M. E., 'Goal setting: a meta-analytic examination of the empirical evidence', *Journal of Applied Psychology*, **71** (1986), pp. 474–83.

16. Mento, A. J. et al., 'A meta-analytic study of the effects of goal setting on task performance: 1966–1984'.

17. Earley, P. C., Wojnaroski, P. and Prest, W., 'Task planning and energy expended: exploration of how goals influence performance', *Journal of Applied Psychology*, **72** (1987), pp. 107–14.

18. See e.g. Larson, J. R., 'The performance feedback process: a preliminary model', *Organizational Behavior and Human Performance*, **33** (1984), pp. 42–76.

19. Source: Podsakoff, P. M., Todor, W. D., Grover, R. A. and Huber, V. L., 'Situational moderators of leader reward and punishment behaviors: fact or fiction?', *Organizational Behavior and Human Performance*, **34** (1984), pp. 21–63.

20. Komaki, J. L., 'Toward effective supervision: an operant analysis and comparison of managers at work', *Journal of Applied Psychology*, **71** (1986), pp. 270–9.

21. Jones, A. P., Tait, M. and Butler, M. C., 'Perceived punishment and reward values of supervisor actions', *Motivation and Emotion*, **7** (1983), p. 321.

22. Komaki, J. L., 'Toward effective supervision'.

23. See e.g. Gioia, D. A. and Sims, H. P., 'Self-serving bias and actor–observer differences in organizations: an empirical analysis', *Journal of Applied Social Psychology*, **15** (1985), pp. 547–63.

24. Mitchell, T. R., Green, S. G. and Wood, R. E., 'An

attributional model of leadership and the poor performing subordinate: development and validation', chapter in Cummings, L. L. and Staw, B. M. (eds.), *Research in Organizational Behavior*, vol. 3 (Greenwich, Connecticut: JAI Press, 1981).

25. Mitchell, T. R., *People in Organizations* (2nd edn., New York McGraw-Hill, 1982), p. 437.

26. Heerwagen, J. H., Beach, L. R. and Mitchell, T. R., 'Dealing with poor performance: supervisor attributions and the cost of responding', *Journal of Applied Social Psychology*, **15** (1985), pp. 638–55.

27. Bryman, A., *Leadership and Organizations*, pp. 111–12.

28. Blanchard, K. and Johnson, S., *The One Minute Manager* (New York: Morrow, 1982).

29. Bryman, A., *Leadership and Organizations*, p. 112.

30. See e.g. Tysoe, M., 'High hopes', *New Society*, 19 April 1984, p. 121.

31. See e.g. Baron, R. A. and Byrne, D., *Social Psychology* (5th edn., Boston: Allyn and Bacon, 1987), p. 180; Terborg, J. R. and Shingledecker, P., 'Employee reactions to supervision and work evaluation as a function of subordinate and manager sex', *Sex Roles*, **9** (1983), pp. 813–24.

32. Jago, A. G. and Vroom, V. H., 'Sex differences in the incidence and evaluation of participative leader behavior', *Journal of Applied Psychology*, **67** (1982), pp. 776–83.

33. Kanter, R. M., *Men and Women of the Corporation* (New York: Basic Books, 1977); Cooper, C. and Davidson, M., *High Pressure* (London: Fontana, 1982); LaRouche, J. and Ryan, R., *Strategies for Women at Work* (London: Unwin, 1984).

34. Baron, R. A., *Behavior in Organizations*, p. 154.

35. Iaffaldano, M. T. and Muchinsky, P. M., 'Job satisfaction and job performance: a meta-analysis', *Psychological Bulletin*, **97** (1985), pp. 251–73.

36. Baron, R. A., *Behavior in Organizations*, pp. 160–2; Locke, E. A. and Henne, D., 'Work motivation theories', chapter in Cooper, C. L. and Robertson, I. (eds.), *International Review of Industrial and Organizational Psychology 1986* (Chichester: John Wiley, 1986), pp. 22–5.

4 Bosses – how to handle them

1. Earle, W. B., Giuliano, T. and Archer, R. L., 'Lonely at the top: the effect of power

on information flow in the dyad', *Personality and Social Psychology Bulletin*, **9** (1983), pp. 629–37.

2. See e.g. Gifford, R., 'Projected interpersonal distance and orientation choices: personality, sex, and social situation', *Social Psychology Quarterly*, **45** (1982), pp. 145–52.

3. Gifford, R., 'Projected interpersonal distance and orientation choices', p. 151.

4. See e.g. Deaux, K. and Wrightsman, L. S., *Social Psychology in the 80s* (4th edn., Monterey, California: Brooks/Cole, 1984), pp. 119–21.

5. Sandler, L., 'The successful and supportive subordinate', *Personnel Journal*, **63** (1984), p. 44.

6. Tjosvold, D., 'Organizational test of goal linkage theory', *Journal of Occupational Behaviour*, **7** (1986), pp. 77–88.

7. *Ibid*.

8. Tjosvold, D., Andrews, R. and Jones, H., 'Cooperative and competitive relationships between leaders and subordinates', *Human Relations*, **36** (1983), pp. 1111–24.

9. Adapted from Argyle, M. and Henderson, M., *The Anatomy of Relationships* (Harmondsworth, Middlesex: Penguin, 1985), p. 262.

10. Musser, S. J., 'A model for predicting the choice of conflict management strategies by subordinates in high-stakes conflicts', *Organizational Behavior and Human Performance*, **29** (1982), pp. 257–69.

11. See Mitchell, T. R., Green, S. G. and Wood, R. E., 'An attributional model of leadership and the poor performing subordinate: development and validation', chapter in Cummings, L. L. and Staw, B. M. (eds.), *Research in Organizational Behavior*, vol. 3 (Greenwich, Connecticut: JAI Press, 1981).

12. McNamara, J. R. and Delamater, R. J., 'Note on the social impact of assertiveness in occupational contexts', *Psychological Reports*, **56** (1985), pp. 819–22.

13. Deaux, K. and Wrightsman, L. S., *Social Psychology in the 80s*, p. 112.

14. Appell, A. L., *A Practical Approach to Human Behavior in Business* (Columbus, Ohio: Charles E. Merrill, 1984), pp. 355–9.

15. Back, K. and Back, K., *Assertiveness at Work* (London: McGraw-Hill, 1982), pp. 57, 58, 66.

16. See Heisler, G. H. and McCormack, J., 'Situational and personality influences on the reception of provocative responses', *Behavior*

Therapy, **13** (1982), pp. 743–50.

17. McNamara, J. R. and Delamater, R. J., 'Note on the social impact of assertiveness in occupational contexts', pp. 819–22.

18. Solomon, L. J., Brehony, K. A., Rothblum, E. D. and Kelly, J. A., 'Corporate managers' reactions to assertive social skills exhibited by males and females', *Journal of Organizational Behavior Management*, **4** (1982), pp. 49–63.

19. McNamara, J. R. and Delamater, R. J., 'Note on the social impact of assertiveness in occupational contexts', p. 820.

20. Heisler, G. H. and McCormack, J., 'Situational and personality influences on the reception of provocative responses'.

21. Kipnis, D., Schmidt, S. M. and Wilkinson, I., 'Intraorganizational influence tactics: explorations in getting one's way', *Journal of Applied Psychology*, **65** (1980), pp. 440–52; Porter, L. W., Allen, R. W. and Angle, H. L., 'The politics of upward influence in organizations', chapter in Cummings, L. L. and Staw, B. M. (eds.), *Research in Organizational Behavior*, vol. 3 (Greenwich, Connecticut: JAI Press, 1981); Schmidt, S.

M. and Kipnis, D., 'Managers' pursuit of individual and organizational goals', *Human Relations*, **37** (1984), pp. 781–94.

22. Adapted from Kipnis, D. et al., 'Intraorganizational influence tactics'.

23. Schilit, W. K. and Locke, E. A., 'A study of upward influence in organizations', *Administrative Science Quarterly*, **27** (1982), pp. 304–16.

24. Cooper, C. and Davidson, M., *High Pressure* (London: Fontana, 1982), p. 82.

25. Kanter, R. M., *Men and Women of the Corporation* (New York: Basic Books, 1977).

26. See e.g. Durkin, K., 'Social cognition and social context in the construction of sex differences', chapter in Baker, M. A. (ed.), *Sex Differences in Human Performance* (Chichester: John Wiley, 1987); Ruble, T. L., Cohen, R. and Ruble, D. N., 'Sex stereotypes: occupational barriers for women', *American Behavioral Scientist*, **27** (1984), pp. 339–56.

27. See also Baron, R. A. and Byrne, D., *Social Psychology* (5th edn., Boston: Allyn and Bacon, 1987), pp. 172–80.

28. LaRouche, J. and Ryan, R., *Strategies for Women at Work* (London: Unwin, 1984).

29. See e.g. Baron, R. A. and

Byrne, D., *Social Psychology*, pp. 514–19.

30. LaRouche, J. and Ryan, R., *Strategies for Women at Work*, pp. 67–8.

5 Decisions – how to make them

1. See e.g. Berkowitz, L., *A Survey of Social Psychology* (3rd edn., New York: Holt, Rinehart and Winston, 1986), p. 105.
2. Gettys, C. F., Pliske, R. M., Manning, C. and Casey, J. T., 'An evaluation of human act generation performance', *Organizational Behavior and Human Decision Processes*, **39** (1987), pp. 23–51.
3. Janis, I. L. and Mann, L., *Decision Making* (New York: Free Press, 1977).
4. See e.g. Wright, G., *Behavioural Decision Theory* (Harmondsworth, Middlesex: Penguin, 1984).
5. Simon, H. A., *Administrative Behavior* (3rd edn., New York: Free Press, 1976).
6. Janis, I. L. and Mann, L., *Decision Making*.
7. Kruglanski, A. W., 'Freeze-think and the Challenger', *Psychology Today*, August 1986, p. 48.
8. Abelson, R. P. and Levi, A., 'Decision making and decision theory', chapter in Lindzey, G. and Aronson, E. (eds.), *Handbook of Social Psychology*, vol. I (3rd edn.,

New York: Random House, 1985), p. 285.
9. *Ibid.*, pp. 289–90.
10. Tversky, A. and Kahneman, D., 'Judgment under uncertainty: heuristics and biases', chapter in Kahneman, D., Slovic, P. and Tversky, A. (eds.), *Judgment under Uncertainty* (Cambridge University Press, 1982).
11. Brockner, J., Nathanson, S., Friend, A., Harbeck, J., Samuelson, C., Houser, R., Bazerman, M. H. and Rubin, J. Z., 'The role of modeling processes in the "knee deep in the Big Muddy" phenomenon', *Organizational Behavior and Human Performance*, **33** (1984), p. 78. See also e.g. Bazerman, M. H., Giuliano, T. and Appelman, A., 'Escalation of commitment in individual and group decision making', *Organizational Behavior and Human Performance*, **33** (1984), pp. 141–52.
12. Kruglanski, A. W., 'Freeze-think and the Challenger', p. 49.
13. Amabile, T. M., 'The social psychology of creativity: a componential conceptualization', *Journal of Personality and Social Psychology*, **45** (1983), pp. 357–76.
14. *Ibid.*, p. 363.
15. Gilhooly, K. J., *Thinking* (London: Academic Press, 1982), p. 135.

16. Boice, R., 'Contingency management in writing and the appearance of creative ideas: implications for the treatment of writing blocks', *Behaviour Research and Therapy*, 21 (1983), pp. 537–43.

17. For more on the four stages see Gilhooly, K. J., *Thinking*, chapter 7.

18. *Ibid.*, p. 133.

19. Perkins, D. N., *The Mind's Best Work* (Cambridge, Massachusetts: Harvard University Press, 1981), pp. 49–58.

20. Gilhooly, K. J., *Thinking*, pp. 135–8.

21. See e.g. Baron, R. A. and Byrne, D., *Social Psychology* (5th edn., Boston: Allyn and Bacon, 1987), pp. 385–7; Berkowitz, L., *A Survey of Social Psychology*, pp. 297–8; Casey, J. T., Gettys, C. F., Pliske, R. M. and Mehle, T., 'A partition of small group predecision performance into informational and social components', *Organizational Behavior and Human Performance*, 34 (1984), pp. 112–39.

22. See e.g. Baron, R. A. and Byrne, D., *Social Psychology*, pp. 391–3.

23. See e.g. Bass, B., 'Individual capability, team performance, and team productivity', chapter in Dunnette, M. D. and Fleishman, E. A. (eds.), *Human Performance and Productivity. Vol. 1: Human Capability Assessment* (Hillsdale, N. J.: Lawrence Erlbaum, 1982); Yetton, P. and Bottger, P., 'The relationships among group size, member ability, social decision schemes, and performance', *Organizational Behavior and Human Performance*, 32 (1983), pp. 145–59.

24. See Bass, B., 'Individual capability, team performance, and team productivity'.

25. Tjosvold, D., Wedley, W. C. and Field, R. H. G., 'Constructive controversy, the Vroom–Yetton model, and managerial decision-making', *Journal of Occupational Behaviour*, 7 (1986), pp. 127, 135.

26. Hemming, H., 'Women in a man's world: sexual harassment', *Human Relations*, 38 (1985), p. 77.

27. Baron, R. A. and Byrne, D., *Social Psychology*, p. 229; Asch, S. G. 'Effects of group pressure upon the modification and distortion of judgment', chapter in Guetzkow, H. (ed.), *Groups, Leadership, and Men* (Pittsburgh: Carnegie, 1951).

28. Berkowitz, L., *A Survey of Social Psychology*, pp. 298–9.

29. For reviews and discussions of group polarization see e.g. Baron, R. A. and Byrne, D., *Social Psychology*, pp. 393–8; Isenberg, D. J., 'Group

polarization: a critical review and meta-analysis', *Journal of Personality and Social Psychology*, 50 (1986), pp. 1141–51; Lloyd, P., Mayes, A., Manstead, A. S. R., Meudell, P. R. and Wagner, H. L., *Introduction to Psychology* (London: Fontana, 1984), pp. 680–3.

30. Baron, R. A., *Behavior in Organizations* (2nd edn., Boston: Allyn and Bacon, 1986), p. 418.

31. The term 'group polarization', rather confusingly, has been used by psychologists in two ways. First, to refer to the finding that group decisions are often more extreme than the average of the members' pre-discussion positions. Second, to mean the discovery that, after group discussion, the initial tendency of group members in a particular direction frequently becomes intensified. In other words, the members' private attitudes change. It has been commonly assumed that the two are inextricably linked; but the connection between the two may not be quite so straightforward (see Hinsz, V. B. and Davis, J. H., 'Persuasive arguments theory, group polarization, and choice shifts', *Personality and Social Psychology Bulletin*, 10 (1984), pp. 260–8). The 'persuasive arguments' and 'social comparison' explanations I put forward in the text have been suggested to account for both phenomena.

32. Stasser, G. and Titus, W., 'Pooling of unshared information in group decision making: biased information sampling during discussion', *Journal of Personality and Social Psychology*, 48 (1985), pp. 1467–78.

33. Janis, I. L., *Victims of Groupthink* (Boston: Houghton Mifflin, 1972); Janis, I. L., *Groupthink* (revised and enlarged edition of *Victims of Groupthink*) (Boston: Houghton Mifflin, 1982).

34. Janis, I. L., 'Counteracting the adverse effects of concurrence-seeking in policy-planning groups: theory and research perspectives', chapter in Brandstätter, H., Davis, J. H. and Stocker-Kreichgauer, G. (eds.), *Group Decision Making* (London: Academic Press, 1982), p. 479.

35. See e.g. Janis, I. L., 'Counteracting the adverse effects of concurrence-seeking in policy-planning groups'.

36. Heller, F., 'The danger of Groupthink', *Guardian*, 31 January 1983.

37. Steiner, I. D., 'Heuristic models of groupthink', chapter in Brandstätter, H. et al., *Group Decision Making*.

38. Irving Janis views this as a crucial factor.

39. Steiner, I. D., 'Heuristic models of groupthink'.

40. Longley, J. and Pruitt, D. G., 'Groupthink: a critique of Janis's theory', chapter in Wheeler, L. (ed.), *Review of Personality and Social Psychology*, vol. 1 (Beverly Hills, California: Sage, 1980); Steiner, I. D., 'Heuristic models of groupthink'.

41. Janis, I. L., 'Counteracting the adverse effects of concurrence-seeking in policy-planning groups', p. 487.

6 *Influence – how to gain it*

1. Cialdini, R. B., *Influence* (New York: William Morrow, 1984), pp. 11, 12.

2. Freedman, J. L. and Fraser, S. C., 'Compliance without pressure: the foot-in-the-door technique', *Journal of Personality and Social Psychology*, 4 (1966), pp. 195–202.

3. Cialdini, R. B., Vincent, J. E., Lewis, S. K., Catalan, J., Wheeler, D. and Darby, B. L., 'Reciprocal concessions procedure for inducing compliance: the door-in-the-face technique', *Journal of Personality and Social Psychology*, 31 (1975), pp. 206–15.

4. Duck, S., *Human Relationships* (London: Sage, 1986), p. 175.

5. Pallak, M. S., Cook, D. A. and Sullivan, J. J., 'Commitment and energy conservation', *Applied Social Psychology Annual*, 1 (1980), pp. 235–53.

6. Cialdini, R. B., *Influence*, p. 101.

7. Duck, S., *Human Relationships*, p. 176.

8. Baron, R. A. and Byrne, D., *Social Psychology* (5th edn., Boston: Allyn and Bacon, 1987), p. 250.

9. *Ibid.*, p. 251.

10. Duck, S., *Human Relationships*, p. 185.

11. See e.g. Deaux, K. and Wrightsman, L. S., *Social Psychology in the 80s* (4th edn., Monterey, California: Brooks/Cole), pp. 323–4.

12. Petty, R. E. and Cacioppo, J. T., *Attitudes and Persuasion* (Dubuque, Iowa: Wm. C. Brown, 1981); Petty, R. E. and Cacioppo, J. T., 'The elaboration likelihood model of persuasion', chapter in Berkowitz, L. (ed.), *Advances in Experimental Social Psychology*, vol. 19 (London: Academic Press, 1986).

13. See Eiser, J. R., *Social Psychology* (Cambridge University Press, 1986), p. 47.

14. Petty, R. E. and Cacioppo, J. T., 'The effects of involvement on responses to argument quantity and quality: central and

peripheral routes to persuasion', *Journal of Personality and Social Psychology*, **46** (1984), p. 70.

15. See e.g. Karlins, M. and Abelson, H. I., *How Opinions and Attitudes are Changed* (2nd edn., New York: Springer, 1970).

16. See e.g. Deaux, K. and Wrightsman, L. S., *Social Psychology in the 80s*, pp. 284–5.

17. Petty, R. E. and Cacioppo, J. T., 'The effects of involvement on responses to argument quantity and quality', pp. 69–81.

18. Valeriani, R., *Travels with Henry* (Boston: Houghton Mifflin, 1979). Quoted in O'Quin, K. and Aronoff, J., 'Humor as a technique of social influence', Social Psychology Quarterly, **44** (1981), p. 355.

19. O'Quin, K. and Aronoff, J., 'Humor as a technique of social influence', pp. 349–57.

20. See e.g. Berkowitz, L., *A Survey of Social Psychology* (3rd edn., New York: Holt, Rinehart and Winston, 1986), pp. 194–5.

21. Eiser, J. R., *Social Psychology*, pp. 48–9; Heesacker, M., Petty, R. E. and Cacioppo, J. T., 'Field dependence and attitude change: source credibility can alter persuasion by affecting message-relevant thinking', *Journal of Personality*, **51** (1983), pp. 653–66.

22. Baron, R. A., *Behavior in Organizations* (2nd edn., Boston: Allyn and Bacon, 1986), p. 143.

23. Eagly, A. H. and Chaiken, S., 'Cognitive theories of persuasion', chapter in Berkowitz, L. (ed.), *Advances in Experimental Social Psychology*, vol. 17 (New York: Academic Press, 1984).

24. Petty, R. E. and Cacioppo, J. T., 'The effects of involvement on responses to argument quantity and quality', p. 70.

25. See e.g. Deutsch, M. and Gerard, H. B., 'A study of normative and informational social influence upon individual judgment,'. *Journal of Abnormal and Social Psychology*, **51** (1955), pp. 629–36.

26. See Moscovici, S., Mugny, G. and Van Avermaet, E. (eds.), *Perspectives on Minority Influence* (Cambridge University Press, 1985); Berkowitz, L., *A Survey of Social Psychology*, pp. 224–7; Maass, A. and Clark, R. D., 'Hidden impact of minorities: fifteen years of minority influence research', *Psychological Bulletin*, **95** (1984), pp. 428–50; Mugny, G., 'The influence of minorities: ten years later', chapter in Tajfel, H. (ed.), *The Social Dimension*, vol. 2 (Cambridge University Press, 1984).

27. Nemeth, C. J., 'Differential contributions of majority and minority influence', *Psychological Review*, **93** (1986), pp. 23–32.

28. See e.g. Maass, A. and Clark, R. D., 'Hidden impact of minorities', p. 438.

29. See e.g. Hollander, E. P., *Principles and Methods of Social Psychology* (4th edn., New York: Oxford University Press, 1981), pp. 241, 244–7; Katz, G. M., 'Previous conformity, status, and the rejection of the deviant', *Small Group Behavior*, **13** (1982), pp. 403–14.

30. Bottger, P. C., 'Expertise and air time as bases of actual and perceived influence in problem-solving groups', *Journal of Applied Psychology*, **69** (1984), pp. 214–21.

31. Source: Hall, J. and Watson, W. H., 'The effects of a normative intervention on group decision-making performance', *Human Relations*, **23** (1970), pp. 316–17.

32. See e.g. Eagly, A. H., 'Gender and social influence: a social psychological analysis', *American Psychologist*, **38** (1983), pp. 971–81; Hollander, E. P., 'Leadership and power', chapter in Lindzey, G. and Aronson, E. (eds.), *The Handbook of Social Psychology*, vol. II (3rd edn., New York: Random House, 1985), pp. 519–23; Webster, M. and Driskell, J. E., 'Processes of status generalization', chapter in Blumberg, H. H., Hare, A. P., Kent, V. and Davies, M. F. (eds.), *Small Groups and Social Interaction*, vol 1 (Chichester: John Wiley, 1983) pp. 64–6; Wood, W. and Karten, S. J., 'Sex differences in interaction style as a product of perceived sex differences in competence', *Journal of Personality and Social Psychology*, **50** (1986), pp. 341–7.

7 Stress – how to beat it

1. See Cherry, N., 'Women and work stress: evidence from the 1946 birth cohort', *Ergonomics*, **27** (1984), pp. 519–26.

2. Warr, P. and Payne, R., 'Affective outcomes of paid employment in a random sample of British workers', *Journal of Occupational Behaviour*, **4** (1983), pp. 91–104.

3. For more on personality and stress see e.g. Lucas, M., Wilson, K. and Hart, E., *How to Survive the 9–5* (London: Thames Methuen, 1986), chapters 3 and 4.

4. Appell, A. L., *A Practical Approach to Human Behavior in Business*

(Columbus, Ohio: Charles E. Merrill, 1984), p. 234.

5. Selye, H., *Stress Without Distress* (Philadelphia: Lippincott, 1974), p. 54. Quoted in Appell, A. L., *A Practical Approach to Human Behavior in Business*, p. 234.

6. See e.g. Atkinson, R. L., Atkinson, R. C. and Hilgard, E. R., *Introduction to Psychology* (8th edn., San Diego: Harcourt Brace Jovanovich, 1983), p. 438.

7. See e.g. Appell, A. L., *A Practical Approach to Human Behavior in Business*, chapter 14; Beech, H. R., Burns, L. E. and Sheffield, B. F., *A Behavioural Approach to the Management of Stress* (Chichester: John Wiley, 1982), pp. 8–14; Lucas, M. et al., *How to Survive the 9–5.*

8. See e.g. Baron, R. A., *Behavior in Organizations*, (2nd edn., Boston: Allyn and Bacon, 1986), pp. 220–1.

9. See e.g. Appell, A. L., *A Practical Approach to Human Behavior in Business*, chapter 14; Cooper, C. and Davidson, M., *High Pressure* (London: Fontana, 1982); Lucas, M. et al., *How to Survive the 9–5.*

10. See e.g. Appell, A. L., *A Practical Approach to Human Behavior in Business*, chapter 14; Beech, H. R. et al., *A Behavioural Approach to the Management of Stress*, pp. 8–14; Cooper, C. and Davidson, M., *High Pressure*; Lucas, M. et al., *How to Survive the 9–5.*

11. Cooper, C. and Davidson, M., *High Pressure*, p. 192.

12. Lucas, M. et al., *How to Survive the 9–5.*

13. See e.g. Baron, R. A., *Behavior in Organizations*, pp. 221–5; Cooper, C. and Davidson, M., *High Pressure.*

14. *Ibid.*, p. 195.

15. Baron, R. A., *Behavior in Organizations*, p. 225.

16. See Cooper, C. and Davidson, M., *High Pressure*, p. 199.

17. See e.g. Baron, R. A., *Behavior in Organizations*, pp. 207–14; Beech, H. R. et al., *A Behavioural Approach to the Management of Stress*, pp. 1–8; Cooper, C. L., *Executive Families Under Stress* (Englewood Cliffs, N.J.: Prentice-Hall, 1981); Cooper, C. L., 'Identifying stressors at work: recent research developments', *Journal of Psychosomatic Research*, 27 (1983), pp. 369–76; Cooper, C. L., 'Stress', chapter in Cooper, C. L. and Makin, P. (eds.), *Psychology for Managers* (London: British Psychological Society/ Macmillan, 1984).

18. Cary Cooper, in conversation with the author, April 1986.

19. Cooper, C. L., 'Job distress: recent research and the emerging role of the clinical

occupational psychologist', *Bulletin of the British Psychological Society*, **39** (1986), p. 329.

20. Firth, J. and Shapiro, D. A., 'An evaluation of psychotherapy for job-related distress', *Journal of Occupational Psychology*, **59** (1986), pp. 111–19.

21. See Aldwin, C. M. and Revenson, T. A., 'Does coping help? A re-examination of the relation between coping and mental health', *Journal of Personality and Social Psychology*, **53** (1987), pp. 337–48.

22. Folkman, S., Lazarus, R. S., Dunkel-Schetter, C., DeLongis, A. and Gruen, R. J., 'Dynamics of a stressful encounter: cognitive appraisal, coping, and encounter outcomes', *Journal of Personality and Social Psychology*, **50** (1986), p. 1001.

23. Latack, J. C., 'Coping with job stress: measures and future directions for scale development', *Journal of Applied Psychology*, **71** (1986), pp. 377–85.

24. Folkman, S. et al., 'Dynamics of a stressful encounter', pp. 992–1003.

25. Aldwin, C. M. and Revenson, T. A., 'Does coping help?'; Folkman, S., Lazarus, R. S., Gruen, R. J. and DeLongis, A., 'Appraisal, coping, health status, and psychological symptoms', *Journal of Personality and Social Psychology*, **50** (1986), pp. 571–9.

26. Source: Folkman, S. et al., 'Dynamics of a stressful encounter', p. 996.

27. See e.g. Kobasa, S. C., Maddi, S. R. and Kahn, S., 'Hardiness and health: a prospective study', *Journal of Personality and Social Psychology*, **42** (1982), pp. 168–77; Kobasa, S. C. O. and Puccetti, M. C., 'Personality and social resources in stress resistance', *Journal of Personality and Social Psychology*, **45** (1983), pp. 839–50.

28. Kobasa, S. C. et al., 'Hardiness and health', p. 170.

29. Folkman, S., 'Personal control and stress and coping processes: a theoretical analysis', *Journal of Personality and Social Psychology*, **46** (1984), pp. 839–52; McCrae, R. R., 'Situational determinants of coping responses: loss, threat, and challenge', *Journal of Personality and Social Psychology*, **46** (1984), pp. 919–28.

30. Scheier, M. F., Weintraub, J. K. and Carver, C. S., 'Coping with stress: divergent strategies of optimists and pessimists', *Journal of Personality and Social Psychology*, **51** (1986), pp. 1257–64.

31. See e.g. Caldwell, R. A., Pearson, J. L. and Chin, R. J., 'Stress-moderating effects: social support in the context of gender and locus of control', *Personality and Social Psychology Bulletin*, 13 (1987), pp. 5–17; Cohen, S. and Wills, T. A., 'Stress, social support, and the buffering hypothesis', *Psychological Bulletin*, 98 (1985), pp. 310–57; Dooley, D., Rook, K. and Catalano, R., 'Job and non-job stressors and their moderators', *Journal of Occupational Psychology*, 60 (1987), pp. 115–32; Ganster, D. C., Fusilier, M. R. and Mayes, B. T., 'Role of social support in the experience of stress at work', *Journal of Applied Psychology*, 71 (1986), pp. 102–10.

32. See e.g. Henderson, M. and Argyle, M., 'Social support by four categories of work colleagues: relationships between activities, stress and satisfaction', *Journal of Occupational Behaviour*, 6 (1985), pp. 229–39.

33. Kobasa, S. C. O. and Puccetti, M. C., 'Personality and social resources in stress resistance', p. 849.

34. See Folkman, S., 'Personal control and stress and coping processes'.

35. Martin, R. A. and Lefcourt, H. M., 'Sense of humor as a moderator of the relation between stressors and moods', *Journal of Personality and Social Psychology*, 45 (1983), pp. 1313–24.

36. See e.g. Krause, N. and Stryker, S., 'Stress and well-being: the buffering role of locus of control beliefs', *Social Science and Medicine*, 18 (1984), pp. 783–90; Parkes, K. R., 'Locus of control, cognitive appraisal, and coping in stressful episodes', *Journal of Personality and Social Psychology*, 46 (1984), pp. 655–68; Zika, S. and Chamberlain, K., 'Relation of hassles and personality to subjective well-being', *Journal of Personality and Social Psychology*, 53 (1987), pp. 155–62.

37. See Folkman, S., 'Personal control and stress and coping processes'.

38. See Folkman, S., 'Personal control and stress and coping processes'; Silver, R. L. and Wortman, C. B., 'Coping with undesirable life events', chapter in Garber, J. and Seligman, M. E. P. (eds.), *Human Helplessness* (New York: Academic Press, 1980).

39. Adapted from Latack, J. C., 'Coping with job stress', p. 380.

40. Kobasa, S. C., 'Commitment and coping in stress resistance among lawyers', *Journal of Personality and Social*

Psychology, **42** (1982), pp. 707–17.

41. Adapted from Aldwin, C. M. and Revenson, T. A., 'Does coping help?', p. 347.

42. See e.g. Lucas, M. et al., *How to Survive the 9–5*, pp. 152–4.

43. See e.g. Beech, H. R. et al., *A Behavioural Approach to the Management of Stress*, chapter 4; Murphy, L. R., 'A comparison of relaxation methods for reducing stress in nursing personnel', *Human Factors*, **25** (1983), pp. 431–40.

44. Source: Appell, A. L., *A Practical Approach to Human Behavior in Business*, p. 239.

45. Source: Lucas, M. et al., *How to Survive the 9–5*, p. 155.

46. See e.g. Lucas, M. et al., *How to Survive the 9–5*, pp. 151–2.

47. Roth, D. L. and Holmes, D. S., 'Influence of physical fitness in determining the impact of stressful life events on physical and psychologic health', *Psychosomatic Medicine*, **47** (1985), pp.164–73.

48. Bethell, H., 'And one for the road', *Sunday Times Magazine*, 8 March 1987.

49. Thayer, R. E., 'Energy, tiredness, and tension effects of a sugar snack versus moderate exercise', *Journal of Personality and Social Psychology*, **52** (1987), pp. 119–25.

50. Baron, R. A., *Behavior in Organizations*, p. 220.

51. Cooper, C. and Davidson, M., *High Pressure*, p. 136.

52. Reynolds, H. and Tramel, M. E., *Executive Time Management* (Aldershot, Hampshire: Wildwood House, 1979), p. 40.

53. Adair, J., *Effective Leadership* (London: Pan, 1983), pp. 155–6.

54. Lucas, M. et al., *How to Survive the 9–5*, p. 157.

55. See e.g. Baron, R. A. and Byrne, D., *Social Psychology* (5th edn., Boston: Allyn and Bacon, 1987), pp. 504–11, 514.

56. Source: Appell, A. L., *A Practical Approach to Human Behavior in Business*, p. 236.

57. Source: Lucas, M. et al., *How to Survive the 9–5*, pp. 67–8.

58. Dembroski, T. M., MacDougall, J. M., Williams, R. B., Haney, T. L. and Blumenthal, J. A., 'Components of Type A, hostility, and anger-in: relationship to angiographic findings', *Psychosomatic Medicine*, **47** (1985), pp. 219–33.

59. See e.g. Dembroski, T. M. et al., 'Components of Type A, hostility, and anger-in'; Fischman, J., 'Type A on trial', *Psychology Today*, February 1987, pp. 42–50; Friedman, H. S. and Booth-Kewley, S., 'Personality, Type A behavior, and coronary heart disease: the role of emotional expression',

Journal of Personality and Social Psychology, **53** (1987), pp. 783–92.
60. Cooper, C. L., 'Job distress', p. 325.

8 Getting it all in perspective

1. Berkowitz, L., *A Survey of Social Psychology* (3rd edn., New York: Holt, Rinehart and Winston, 1986), p. 97.
2. Quoted in Weiner, B., 'An attributional theory of achievement motivation and emotion', *Psychological Review*, **92** (1985), p. 548.
3. See e.g. Baron, R.A. and Byrne, D., *Social Psychology* (5th edn., Boston: Allyn and Bacon, 1987), pp. 59–62.
4. See e.g. Baron, R. A., *Behavior in Organizations* (2nd edn., Boston: Allyn and Bacon, 1986), pp. 118–19.
5. Ward, C. H. and Eisler, R. M., 'Type A behavior, achievement striving, and a dysfunctional self-evaluation system', *Journal of Personality and Social Psychology*, **53** (1987), pp. 318–26.
6. See e.g. Eiser, J. R., *Social Psychology* (Cambridge University Press, 1986), pp. 202–3.
7. See e.g. Baron, R. A. and Byrne, D., *Social Psychology*, pp. 63–4; Försterling, F., 'Attributional retraining: a review', *Psychological*

Bulletin, **98** (1985), pp. 495–512; Trotter, R. J., 'Stop blaming yourself', *Psychology Today*, February 1987, pp. 31–9; Weiner, B., 'An attributional theory of achievement motivation and emotion', pp. 548–73.
8. Cooper, C. and Davidson, M., *High Pressure* (London: Fontana, 1982), pp. 136–7.
9. See e.g. Duck, S., *Human Relationships* (London: Sage, 1986).
10. See e.g. Lewis, S. N. C. and Cooper, C. L., 'Stress in two-earner couples and stage in the life-cycle', *Journal of Occupational Psychology*, **60** (1987), pp. 289–303.
11. Source: The Henley Centre for Forecasting, *Leisure Futures*, summer 1986. Quoted in Central Statistical Office, *Social Trends*, no. 17 (London: Her Majesty's Stationery Office, 1987), p. 163.
12. See e.g. Cooper, C. L., 'Problem areas for future stress research: cancer and working women', chapter in Cooper, C. L. (ed.), *Stress Research* (Chichester: John Wiley, 1983), pp. 112–14.
13. Haynes, S. G. and Feinleib, M., 'Women, work and coronary heart disease: prospective findings from the Framingham Heart Study', *American Journal of Public Health*, **70** (1980), pp. 133–41. Quoted in

Cooper, C. L., 'Problem areas for future stress research', p. 112.

14. See e.g. Cooper, C. L., 'Problem areas for future stress research', p. 112.

15. See also Lewis, C. and O'Brien, M. (eds.), *Reassessing Fatherhood* (London: Sage, 1987).

16. Baruch, G. K. and Barnett, R. C., 'Consequences of fathers' participation in family work: parents' role strain and well-being', *Journal of Personality and Social Psychology*, **51** (1986), pp. 983–92.

17. *Ibid.*, p. 990.

18. See e.g. Cooper, C. L., 'Job distress: recent research and the emerging role of the clinical occupational psychologist', *Bulletin of The British Psychological Society*, **39** (1986), pp. 325–31.

19. Lucas, M., Wilson, K. and Hart, E., *How to Survive the 9–5* (London: Thames Methuen, 1986), p. 139.

20. Cooper, C. and Davidson, M., *High Pressure*, p. 153.

21. Cooper, C. L., *Executive Families Under Stress* (Englewood Cliffs, N.J.: Prentice-Hall, 1981), pp. 114, 116.

22. Linville, P. W., 'Self-complexity as a cognitive buffer against stress-related illness and depression', *Journal of Personality and Social Psychology*, **52** (1987), pp. 663–76.

INDEX

What They Don't Teach You at Harvard Business School

Mark H. McCormack

Mark McCormack, founder of the sports management industry and now manager and marketer of achievement in such diverse forms as Martina Navratilova, Sebastian Coe and Jack Nicklaus, is a legendarily successful entrepreneur. His knowledge of selling, marketing and management is second to none.

Now, for the first time, he reveals the secrets of his business success in a book which – like him – is sharp, precise and very much to the point. It fills the gap between a business school education and the street knowledge that comes from the day-to-day experience of running a business and managing people.

The collected wisdom, golden rules and unorthodox advice he offers is guaranteed to make anyone's professional life more successful. As he himself says: 'It's all based on my experience, so I know it works.'

FONTANA PAPERBACKS

Fontana Paperbacks
Non-fiction

Fontana is a leading paperback publisher of non-fiction.
Below are some recent titles.

Armchair Golf *Ronnie Corbett* £3.50
You Are Here *Kevin Woodcock* £3.50
Squash Balls *Barry Waters* £3.50
Men: An Owner's Manual *Stephanie Brush* £2.50
Impressions of My Life *Mike Yarwood* £2.95
Arlott on Wine *John Arlott* £3.95
Beside Rugby *Bill Beaumont* £3.50
Agoraphobia *Robyn Vines* £3.95
The Serpent and the Rainbow *Wade Davies* £2.95
Alternatives to Drugs *Colin Johnson & Arabella Melville* £4.95
The Learning Organization *Bob Garratt* £3.95
Information and Organizations *Max Boisot* £3.50
Say It One Time For The Broken Hearted *Barney Hoskins* £4.95
March or Die *Tony Geraghty* £3.95
Nice Guys Sleep Alone *Bruce Feirstein* £2.95
Royal Hauntings *Joan Forman* £3.50
Going For It *Victor Kiam* £2.95
Sweets *Shona Crawford Poole* £3.95
Waugh on Wine *Auberon Waugh* £3.95

You can buy Fontana paperbacks at your local bookshop or newsagent.
Or you can order them from Fontana Paperbacks, Cash Sales Department, Box 29, Douglas, Isle of Man. Please send a cheque, postal or money order (not currency) worth the purchase price plus 22p per book for postage (maximum postage required is £3).

NAME (Block letters) _____

ADDRESS _____

_____

_____